No Ordinary OWL

Lauraine Snelling *and*
Kathleen Damp Wright

No Ordinary OWL

Lauraine Snelling *and*
Kathleen Damp Wright

the
S.A.V.E.
Squad

BARBOUR
PUBLISHING

Dedication

To Cami M., Evan and Naomi W. and Natalie A.
Looking forward to buying your books one day.

Heartfelt thanks to Annie Rose for the exquisite
sculptures of each animal in the series.

Acknowledgments

Thanks most especially to Julie, Alex, and Natalie for
night-vision goggle drills in their backyard, and to Daniel for
letting me borrow his. Students are indeed the gifts that keep
on giving. Becky, for naming the book during a Bossy Girls
lunch. Corinne K., for the pickle story. Dalyn at Utah Wildlife
Rehabilitation of Utah Center, for both her time and the work she
and her faithful volunteers do for the wild ones. The Tracy Aviary,
for lovely places to learn about all things avian.

Always to my husband, Fred, for his support.

Always to You, Jesus, for being our wind,
our wings, and our guiding light.

Chapter 1

Melissa's Menacing Message

Where *are* they? Eleven-year-old Esther Martin began to wonder if the rest of the S.A.V.E. Squad was going to show up at the community center on this rainy Saturday. But they had *promised*.

Large, draped dog crates sat along the stage. "We'll be beginning our bird show in just a few minutes. I'll be introducing you to Beverly Beake, a licensed bird educator and rehabber for wild birds." The short, round mayor of Oakton City paused and stuck the mic closer to her mouth to whisper, "But not the little birds you're thinking of!" She stepped off the stage.

A bird lady named *Beake*. Snorting with amusement, Esther snuck another quick look back toward the doors. This very auditorium was where Esther, Vee, Sunny, and Aneta first found out they'd won spots as Junior Event Planners for a city festival. Way back in the summer. Before they even liked each other. Now Monday would be Spring Break, and the Squad would have a whole week together.

She loved everything about being a member of the S.A.V.E. Squad. Sunny, Aneta, and Vee. The serious-minded, dark-haired, and dark-eyed list maker, Vee. Spinning Sunny with the red hair, freckles, and friendly smile. Blue-eyed, blond-haired Aneta who loved her adoptive home with her lawyer mom. These girls liked her. Even when she was prickly. Sometimes she *could* be prickly. But only when she was right and nobody was listening. They teased her about her need to be right and her love of the Internet. It was the first time she'd had friends. Like this, anyway. Esther gave another little hop in her seat and glanced back. She wanted the Squad to be together always and continue their wild adventures.

A whoosh of air lifted the back of her hair as someone flopped next to her. Esther turned to say the seats were *saved*—because all three were protected by her fierce glare, her bike helmet, and her wet raincoat. Her eyes widened.

"Hello, Esther. Oh, ew, just saying, but with your mouth hanging open? You look like you have three chins instead of two." The girl with brown hair delicately highlighted and a perfect French manicure regarded her with what Aneta called "The Melissa Smile." It was not a friendly smile. It meant that she was sizing you up, all the better to eat you.

"M–Melissa." Melissa Dayton-Snipp was not supposed to be in Oakton, Oregon. Aneta, who had endured Melissa at the girls' private school last year, had been happy to report at the start of school that Melissa had flown to France to attend a fancy horse-riding school.

"In about a week and a half April will arrive, a lovely time of year here in Oakton." The mayor was back on stage. As always, her scratchy voice boomed as though she were introducing the most exciting thing on the planet. "Don't you love the changes that come with each new spring?" The mayor directed her question to the tall, thin woman who stood next to her. With her neck slightly humped and horns on the corners of her glasses, she looked like the turkey buzzard Esther had researched for her recent extra-credit science project. Yes, the one she got an A on. The woman's nose resembled the turkey buzzard a bit with its sharp hook, yet the woman's eyes, even seen from the second row, were friendly. Her wide, thin-lipped mouth was smiling. She nodded in response to the mayor's question.

The mayor glanced out at the crowd. "Don't you all love the changes of spring, too?"

Not really, Esther thought in a panic, while Melissa, other kids, and parents nodded their heads. *She* didn't want anything to change. Life was perfect as part of the S.A.V.E. Squad. Melissa showing up only proved that change was not good.

"How come you're back?" Esther managed to choke some words out. *Wait until Aneta shows up. Aneta will freak.*

Looking down her nose at Esther, Melissa smoothed her perfect hair. "I am recovering from an unfortunate accident at *École D'élite Pour Des Cavaliers.*" She rolled the name of the French riding school off her tongue like she said it a lot. Which, Esther thought, she probably did. Even to people who didn't care. *Like me.*

Then, craning her neck past Melissa at the empty row, Esther continued, "Where are all your friends?" She meant "servants," as Melissa ran a group of girls who dressed like Melissa, acted like Melissa—*shudder*—and talked like Melissa. They followed the Rules of Melissa or risked nobody talking to them.

"*Those* girls?" Melissa's curled lip indicated Esther had been living in a cave or was stupid. Or both. "Nothing stays the same."

"The Squad does." Esther knew as soon as she said it that she should have kept it in her head.

Melissa cocked her head and flicked her tongue along her perfect white teeth, like a snake flicking its forked tongue. "Hmm. Yes, well."

Back in their first adventure, once Sunny, Aneta, Vee, and Esther joined forces to save Wink, an adorable basset hound, they had discovered that their success made Melissa look bad. Melissa hated anyone who made her look bad.

Where are you guys? Esther twisted in her seat. She needed the S.A.V.E. Squad to help her not be afraid of Melissa. Around Melissa, she felt fat, ugly, and stupid. And she knew she wasn't at least *two* of those things.

"Like I said, Esther. I'm moving on." She stood and leaned in close to Esther. "Even the S.A.V.E. Squad could change." She pushed past Esther's knees and was lost in the last-minute bustle of people finding seats.

As sure as she was sitting in the second row, and as sure as she knew that macaroni and cheese was her favorite food, she knew why Melissa had lasered in on her with her snaky smile.

She wants to change the S.A.V.E. Squad.

An icy finger dripped chills that ran down her neck to her feet and pooled there, freezing her toes.

Chapter 2

Lightning Strikes

Esther." Vee frowned as she walked with her friend toward the bike stand outside the community center. "Did you even hear anything the Bird Lady said?" She shook back her glossy black hair and clipped on a green-and-white helmet.

"Hurry, guys! The rain has stopped, and my parents said we could ride bikes to Uncle Dave's if it did, so let's roll!" Sunny was impatient, as always.

Esther had remained stunned as the rest of the Squad arrived, and, because they were in the second row, she couldn't whisper about Melissa's threat. Vee and Aneta had slid into their seats, removed their wet raincoats, and squeezed Esther's hand, just as the Bird Lady began her presentation. Sunny had been late, causing all heads—including the Bird Lady's—to turn toward her as she sprinted to the girls.

"You didn't even say anything when the Bird Lady asked if anyone knew what the birds of prey were called." Sunny was riding in circles in the emptying parking lot.

"You already told us they were raptors, and these raptors weren't dinosaurs," Aneta chimed in, stepping to her bike, helmet and raincoat in place. Squeezing her brakes to test them, she added, "Hooray for a Squad sleepover tonight at Sunny's Uncle Dave's house!"

Esther cleared her throat. "I was in shock." She sucked in a deep breath before they could ask why and said, "Melissa is back!"

She waited for the reaction.

"She's in France." Vee climbed on her bike, pushed off, and began to pedal.

"Lovely, faraway France," Aneta said happily, pedaling after her.

"C'mon. We've got to beat Uncle Dave to the ranch." Sunny zipped by on her bike. "If he beats us from leaving Aneta's house, we have to muck stalls tonight."

Climbing on her bike, Esther wanted to shout that they needed to *listen* to her, that Melissa was *back*. Then, after Sunny's words zapped her mind, she began to pedal. Mucking stalls versus insisting the girls listen to her right now? She'd tell them at the ranch. Quickly snapping up her raincoat, Esther pushed away Melissa's threat. The Squad would know what to do about Melissa.

With Sunny and Vee out in front, Esther pedaled next to Aneta. Two side by side was the max when riding the wide road shoulder out to Uncle Dave's ranch. She sent a smile toward Aneta. While Aneta could smoke both Vee and Sunny with her swimmer's legs, she gave no sign of wanting to leave Esther as the slowest and last in line. Two by two. Squad rule for bike riding. That and helmets. Always. Like Vee said, "I plan on using my brains for a very long time. I want to keep them in my head."

Was that a growl of thunder? Esther squinted at the sky. The afternoon brightness that had followed them out of the parking lot now skittered away to hide behind gloomy clouds. It reminded her of how the mention of Melissa's name *gloomified* everything. Good thing they had their raincoats. A ways up on the right was the haunted mansion with the creepy black-iron fence and giant gate. Once they passed that, only one other driveway on the right remained, then a left turn off the road and they were home free for the fast pedal to Secondhand Horse Ranch and fun. They'd spend the night and then go to Esther's church together tomorrow.

"I love sleepovers at Dave's ranch. We get to play with all the animals." How Aneta could look dreamy eyed and still keep her bike on the road, Esther couldn't imagine. If Esther had been daydreaming like that, she'd be off in the ditch.

After they left the city streets behind and fewer and fewer houses dotted the country road, Esther called for a rest. Although she hated to, because she was slowest of all of them, but she was going to fall over if she didn't. She'd never catch up with them. Aneta accelerated and brought back Sunny and Vee, who were speeding along out of earshot.

"Hey, a stop works for me." Vee pulled the top up on her water bottle and took a swig. "Guess what? You'll never guess the big surprise and change coming to *my* house. I didn't even believe it at first."

Change? That word again. What could Vee's news be? By the way Vee was holding back a flat-out grin from shooting across her face, Esther knew it must be an award at school. Vee attended the Accelerated Learning Center at Moby Perkins Elementary School. Vee liked to think she was the smartest Squad member. Esther wasn't sure, since she herself was always on the high honor roll at Oakton Victory Academy *and* the sixth-grade computer coordinator. *Maybe we're just the smartest at different things.*

"My mom is having a baby!" Vee burst out, not waiting for guesses.

13

Shrieks erupted from all four girls, their voices spilling down the deserted road. The sun jumped out briefly as though celebrating with them.

Esther shrugged in the warmth. "Your mom! Bill will be the coolest dad!" Vee's stepdad, Bill, worked on huge diesels and had a garage at home that the girls were convinced had secret treasure. The trouble was, they weren't allowed in it. Only Vee, and only once when she had convinced Bill to let her organize it. Vee reported there were some high-potential boxes to investigate, labeled "other jobs" that were steel suitcases strapped and locked.

"I have a surprise, too!" Aneta's blue eyes were shining with her secret. "My mom—I think"—Aneta turned to Sunny—"likes your uncle Dave a lot."

"Really?" Sunny's exaggerated looks at Esther and Vee put a furrow in Aneta's brow. "Ready, girls?"

"What took you so long?" The three shouted so piercingly it set off an echo with "longggg, ongggg, onnggggg!"

Their friend look confused. "I do not understand." When Aneta was uncertain or frightened, her English took a dive. Otherwise, their Ukrainian transplant friend did great with her English. Especially after Melissa Dayton-Snipp left Cunningham Preparatory Academy. Having Melissa gone had been good for everyone, in Esther's opinion. Since everyone was telling news, now was a good time to tell the girls Melissa was back.

"We knew it during the last adventure!" Esther said. Well, she'd been the third to know, but still, she'd known before Aneta. Sunny and Vee had been shooting sideways looks at each other. At first, Esther thought they were having a secret and leaving Esther and Aneta out, but then she'd seen how Sunny's uncle—never married—and Aneta's never-married mom spent a lot of time laughing and talking at Uncle Dave's ranch.

"Tell us why you think they like each other," Vee said. "I'm an expert, since Mom and Bill got together."

The furrow disappeared between Aneta's eyes when she smiled. "He calls my mom every day after she gets home from work. He comes over to eat dinner with us a lot, and"—the blue eyes turned from bright blue to dark—"my mom is making a *lot* of peanut butter cookies!"

"It must be true!" Sunny spun.

Esther smothered a laugh. Whenever Aneta's mother had something big to think about, she made peanut butter cookies. During the girls' first adventure, Aneta had gone to sleep several nights with the smell of baking cookies in her nose. It was the only time Aneta's mother cooked. Usually Aneta's grandmother brought over meals to bless Aneta's mom who worked hard as a lawyer.

Opening her mouth to spill the news that would be more giant than either of those changes—*Melissa is back!*—Esther was interrupted by Sunny.

"Well, my parents changed their mind and said if you guys had Spring Break, I could, too!" Sunny was homeschooled.

"The rest of this school year is going to be great." Vee seemed so happy with the change that was coming to her house. Aneta and Sunny, too. Esther wasn't so sure about her house. She suspected something was up at home, and it couldn't be good. Mom was cleaning more than usual, and Dad was snapping orders when he was home. Which wasn't much, since he pastored a church.

"I love us!" She interrupted Sunny who was telling how her brother had been busted while making the family lunch. He'd been biting tiny bites of sweet pickle and spitting them into the tuna salad because he wasn't allowed to use a knife.

Aneta turned a grimacing face to Esther. "What did you say,

Esther? That is so gross, Sunny. I will *never* eat tuna salad again."

"I said I love us," Esther repeated, putting her water bottle back in the bracket. "I hope we stay the S.A.V.E. Squad forever, saving the world one animal at a time." It seemed crummy to tell such bad Melissa news along with everyone's *good* news. She hesitated.

"We'll always be the S.A.V.E. Squad, but we haven't had an animal rescue since forever." Vee played with the strap of her helmet. "It's not like these kinds of birds we saw at the bird show are going to show up for us to help."

The girls laughed, Esther the hardest. *Sure.* A turkey buzzard, a peregrine falcon, and some bird she couldn't remember. She'd taken a quick look at them before the show was over. No cuddling those wild ones.

"Ready to head for the ranch?" Sunny stood poised, her right foot on the pedal and her left foot ready to push off.

"Ready!" sang out Esther. This sleepover would be the official beginning to Spring Break. As soon as they got to the ranch, she'd tell the girls about Melissa. For sure.

A slight bend in the road curved them right, and the black wrought-iron fence began, twisted with the underbrush of winter. Some of it leaned crazily outward like medieval spikes. Esther shivered, not sure if it was because the temperature was dropping or because they were now passing the *way tall* double gate with the big padlock and some square box with buttons on it. Two hulking metal bird sculptures crouched on top of the tallest spikes. The whole entrance looked like a scene out of a scary story when stupid kids investigated where they had no business going.

Plunged immediately away from the gate, the many-puddled dirt driveway disappeared into a dark overhang of evergreen and bare-branched trees. Vee's mom, who was a real-estate agent, had told the girls a Victorian mansion stood at the end of that road. She'd seen it when it was up for sale a few years ago. Back before the mysterious man nobody ever saw—and it was rumored, *hated children*—bought it. Another shiver chilled Esther and, glancing over at Aneta who was also darting glances at the gate, said, "Let's hurry. I'm cold. That place is creepy."

"It looks like ghosts live there," Aneta said, pushing more firmly on her pedals.

An unearthly scream split the air. It began loudly and then tapered away to a screechy gasp.

"What"—Esther said, running off the road into the dirt, narrowly missing the ditch,—"was that?"

"It must be one of the ghosts!"

"There's no such thing as ghosts." Even though Esther knew she was right, it didn't stop her from getting back on and pumping her bike pedals.

In seconds they had caught up to Sunny and Vee.

The redhead circled her bike to swoop by Aneta and Esther. "We made it past the haunted house without getting sucked in by the ghosts!" Her usual mischievous grin preceded a big giggle, and she was off again.

"You didn't hear the scream?" Aneta asked.

Sunny gave her a funny look as she rolled past to ride just a bit in front of Vee. "We're living the yayness!"

I bet she can't tell if Aneta is joking or not. Watching Sunny and Vee, Esther knew exactly what Vee would do, and she did. Standing up on her pedals, the long-legged and fastest runner of the Squad pumped twice, caught up to the shorter girl, and kept juuuusssst a tiny bit ahead of Sunny. Vee liked to win.

"Living the yayness!" Esther grinned and threw a look over her shoulder. A truck was a long way back. She pedaled harder. "Let's pass Sunny and Vee, Aneta. That truck is a long ways back. I bet Sunny and Vee think we're slower than frozen honey!" She glanced over at her friend. "Ready, set, stand, and pump it!"

She and Aneta stood on their pedals, laughing at their flapping rain slickers.

"We are flying now!" Aneta hollered, her long blond ponytail flopping like a horse tail. "I hope we do not get rained on." She pumped easily while Esther puffed.

I want us to live the yayness of the S.A.V.E. Squad when we're a hundred and eighty years old.

They pumped, laughed, and almost caught up to Sunny and Vee when a thunderclap shattered their laughter into shrieks.

When had it turned like almost night? The wind, which had been behind them, viciously folded in on itself and now shoved at them, daring Esther and Aneta to gain any further ground. Heavy raindrops fell, some so big they hurt when they smacked on Esther's helmet, some slipping between the air vents. "Ow!"

Lightning. Lightning. What were you supposed to do when the sky spit bolts of lightning? Besides not be outside. Esther mentally scrambled through memories of fifth-grade weather camp.

Another bolt split the sky. Esther counted, but no thunder followed. She stopped at ten. This was good. Her dad had taught her that counting the seconds between a lightning bolt and a thunder boom told you how many miles away the full storm was. Count three seconds, and the rain was three miles away. *Counting storms,* she thought, wishing Uncle Dave's ranch was closer, *is more fun when you're on a back porch watching it.*

Crrrrr-accckkkk! Another bolt.

Aneta screamed, her face furrowed in fear as she turned a wet face to Esther. "What do we *do*?"

Sunny turned and yelled something like "Pedal for all you're worth!" or maybe it was "Get down in the dirt"?

"There's a ditch by that big tree! We can hide there!" Vee leaped off her bike, tripped on the gravel, and tumbled toward the edge of the shallow ditch, her bike falling with her. Or rather, on top of her.

"Vee!" Aneta, Sunny, and Esther screeched.

"I'm okay, I'm okay." Her face twisted—probably so she wouldn't cry. Vee stood up and brushed herself off. "I think I'll live." Her clean jeans now had muddied knees. The palms of her hands were muddy and scraped. "C'mon, let's lie down in here so we're not the tallest things on the road."

That was it. Now Esther remembered.

I mean, that's not it.

Weather camp: *Never, never lie down in a ditch when there's lightning.* That scrap of memory ejected itself from the past into the now. The wind was picking up. She had to shout to be heard. "No, don't lie down!" They were supposed to get into a car, roll up the windows, and not touch the sides of the car.

Except they didn't have a car.

The girls were looking at her, expecting her to have a better idea. After all, she was the Internet expert.

Squeezing her brakes, Esther stopped so suddenly her back tire skittered a bit. With a big wobble of the handlebars, she managed to get her feet down and keep the rest of her standing up. *Away from trees?* There was nothing *but* trees. Trees on either side of the road. Trees over that creepy black fence. Trees as far as she could see across the road.

"No, don't lie down in the ditch!" Her breath came in gasps. Uncle Dave's ranch was still out of sight on the road that began at the community center and wound its way as a country road. About the only ones who drove it were the people who lived in the sparsely dotted homes, farms, and ranches. Boy, did they need help now. "Help, Lord!"

The first rumble of thunder sounded like a giant's stomach had just decided it was lunchtime. Heavy drops screamed for a few more of their fat friends, and in the time it took Esther to scan for a spot with no trees, the girls' legs and feet were sopping. If they hadn't quickly tied the hoods of the many-colored raincoats, they would look like they'd just washed their hair.

"We look like M&M heads," Sunny said.

Flash! *One–two–three–four*—BOOM!

Aneta screamed.

Vee jumped.

Sunny laughed. "I think my ribs rattled!"

Esther needed a plan to help her friends.

In the next moment, while they crouched near the side of the road away from the big bare tree that leaned over the black fence, the air stilled. Solitary still. Scary still. Like nature had sucked in a bottomless breath and held the planet hostage. A tingle shivered through Esther. *Whoa. What was that?*

Thwaaack! Not a pop, not a thud. *Something hit by something else.*

"My cousin's car!" Sunny shouted, looking around.

"It's a gun!" Vee flattened herself on the ground.

Aneta and Sunny joined her. "Esther, get down!"

Esther dropped so fast dirt went up her nose.

A rustle in the overarching branches of the big tree made them look up in time to see two objects, one larger than the other, dropping fast in front of their faces.

Two pairs of round yellow eyes; wings spread awkwardly; wide-open, sharply curved beaks hissing; and a strange sound that could not be mistaken for anything other than pain.

And blood. Blood on the feathers. Blood on the ground.

Chapter 3

The Man with the Mask

*A*neta screamed.

Vee pulled her hood up until it covered her eyes. "What is that?"

"Blood. There's blood!" Sunny scooted back from the two owls.

"Are they dead?" Esther watched. One wasn't. It twitched and flopped. The other was still, raindrops denting the feathers. Dead?

Aneta crawled forward on her elbows toward the two big-eyed owls. Yellow eyes the size of dimes. "Oh, the poor things are hurt!"

The sharp-looking beak opened farther. Another hiss. Another flop with the brown, white, and gray feathers.

Vee threw back her hood and crouched by the two birds. While the storm continued to jolt and pour, Esther didn't know what to do. But she did know if they didn't get somewhere safe, both the girls and the owls would be dead. She cast another look back down the road.

The truck! It had stopped at the big black fence. Peering through the sheets of rain that pelted her raincoat so loudly she couldn't tell what the other Squaders were talking about, she gauged the distance between the tree and the truck. Could they dodge the lightning if they sprinted? Was a moving target harder for lightning to hit? She turned back to the other three who were circled around the birds.

"Should we pick them up and take them for help?" Aneta reached out a hand toward the less-bloody bird. The beak stretched open. Even though they were small, their wingspread was easily as long as Esther's arm. Maybe longer.

"I say we go get help." Vee's dark, wet bangs stuck to her forehead. She pulled up the hood again. She looked ready to run wherever.

Esther surveyed the two birds, the one still unmoving. If they left them here, they'd drown in the rain. She shivered. The temperature had dropped again, and suddenly her school sweatshirt under the raincoat wasn't warm enough. Maybe the owls would freeze. Those little bodies couldn't take the cold, wet ground.

The gate hadn't opened yet. Someone must still be in the truck. That someone had just been named a helper to the S.A.V.E. Squad. "We'll get the people in the truck to help. The birds are too big for us."

"This would have been a great time for the Anti-Trouble Phone," Vee grumbled, looking disgusted. "I wish I hadn't left it at home."

They agreed. Esther shot a glance at the truck and then up at the gray sky that delivered a never-ending supply of water. Her teeth began to chatter. Oh, she was cold. And wet. And, well, all kinds of scared.

Cr-rrr-ack!

The thunder banged in the sky, and her lungs rattled again. She pulled off her raincoat, threw it over the owls, and ran for the truck.

Vee and Sunny reached the truck first. Esther expected one of them to pound on the driver's side window and scream for help, but that was not what redheaded Sunny did. Reaching the side of the vehicle, she yanked open the passenger side and launched herself into the backseat.

"Sunny!" Vee screeched and stopped short. "What are you doing?"

Another vicious crack of lightning, and Vee joined Sunny.

"Where's the driver?" Esther heard Vee say.

Bang! More lightning. Aneta dove into the truck on top of Vee.

Her teeth chattering, Esther remained outside, unsure. Where was the driver? They were crazy. *We're talking major stranger danger here.* Everything she'd ever learned about safety flashed through her head along with the booms of thunder and flashes of lightning.

Yow! This had to be a special case. She flung open the driver's door and leaped in, slamming it behind her.

Nobody said a word. In seconds, their gasping had steamed up the windows so the truck's interior felt like a sweaty cave.

Outside, the lightning flashed, the thunder boomed, and the pounding sheets of rain fell.

"If the gate's not open, where's the driver?" Vee wanted to know, pulling herself out from under Aneta and squishing Sunny into the door in the process.

"Maybe this is a ghost truck, and the driver is a ghost." Aneta's voice trembled.

Sunny grunted and gasped, "Okay, I think this is the worst trouble the S.A.V.E. Squad has ever been in."

Vee eventually wriggled herself upright as the others straightened themselves. Staring straight ahead at the fence and headlights, Vee nodded. "We've just jumped into some strange truck where nobody is driving during a killer rainstorm, leaving two hurt owls."

The raincoat by the tree hadn't moved. "Lord, we're in big trouble," Esther said. "If the truck is running and the lights are on, someone has to be *somewhere* to help us help those little owls."

A small voice said from the backseat, "We look like we took a shower with our clothes on." It was Aneta. Twisting around to see her, Esther watched her friend's face tremble, and for a moment, Esther thought she was going to cry. Instead her blue eyes crinkled, and her mouth followed with a quivering smile then a choking laugh.

Sunny bent her head as her shoulders shook. "Bahahaha! I feel like a *dog* in a shower!" Shaking like a dog, her tangled mess of curls flung raindrops on the front and back seat, her laughter gaining speed and volume until she was seriously hooting.

"Hey!" Vee frowned. "Getting help for the owls is—" Her stern look wobbled, and she pitched off into a silent fit of hilarity.

This is crazy. Esther felt a bubble of laughter beginning. Why were they laughing? The bubbles were beginning to hurt. She was going to laugh. No she wasn't. Somebody had to be in charge here.

Each of the other three was now soundlessly shaking with mirth. In another second she would join them. It was that kind of laughter after something so scary happened you couldn't deal. She leaned against the cool, fogged-up window, trying to make herself take a breath. Someone had to have a plan. Her face felt like it was on fire, so she turned her face to the glass.

Esther screamed.

The door fell away from her face, and she scrabbled with the steering wheel to stay in the truck. A hard clamp on her arm made her scream again.

"Esther!" the girls were shouting. "What's wrong?" Vee was climbing to the front until her bent right knee locked, leaving her stuck between the two front seats. "Let her alone!" If the Vee Stare could be a voice, Vee was using it now.

A green military slicker yanked Esther out of the truck. The rain had slacked off to mist. She was so cold, so wet.

"What do you want? Why are you in my truck?"

Esther looked in the face of her assailant. A mask. He was wearing a mask. Her voice dried up.

Tears gushed from Esther's eyes, and she began to gulp, feeling more scared than she'd been in her life. "H–h–help the baby owls. . . over—" Deeper sobs took over. She couldn't finish. Vee had untangled her legs now, made the front seat, and in another second shot from the truck, aiming her helmeted head toward the tall, skinny man's stomach.

Chapter 4

Attempts to Escape

They'd blown their first chance for escape. Except, had they really, wondered Esther, since they didn't know they would need to escape? Everything happened so *fast*.

Never had she seen someone move as quickly as that man. Vee made full contact, and while her helmet remained embedded in the masked man's slickered front, he'd grabbed her by the shoulder of her raincoat and Esther by the arm. He'd shoved them in the back with Sunny and Aneta, who had gone deathly silent. Vee was still dizzy from the head butt and complied. Esther's legs quivered like jelly. She obeyed.

They watched the man grab a dog crate from the covered back of the truck and gently scoop up the owls in towels that he pulled from the crates. Then the crate went into the back. The man got in, and there they were.

Kidnapped.

As the truckload of unhappy girls, unhappy owls, and unhappy masked man bounced through the water-filled potholes leading away from safety and toward the haunted mansion, Esther, behind the driver, wanted another look at his face. It was a strange kind of mask. It was clear and kind of smeared his face a little. Openings showed his nose and lips. She also wanted to memorize it so once they escaped, she could tell the sheriff. For, if she knew her S.A.V.E. Squad girls, Vee was plotting and Sunny was plotting. Aneta was hoping that the other three would do something brave. *Now.*

After one particularly deep hole that jounced everyone right, sending Esther into Vee and Vee into Aneta, who in turn smashed Sunny into the door.

The masked man muttered something about "fixing this good."

Uh, Lord?

"You'd better let us out," Sunny announced. "Vee gets major carsick. Esther, trade with Vee so she can have the window for when she hurls." As she spoke, Sunny shoved Aneta and whispered, "Go between Esther and Vee." Moving her long legs, Aneta hitched under Esther as Esther sprawled across the two girls on her way to Sunny's side. What was Sunny up to?

Vee shot to rigidly upright. "I do n——," she began. Aneta jammed an elbow into her ribs.

"Poor Vee does not ride good." The English wasn't so great, but Aneta was terrified and that's when her English flew out the window.

"Oh, I do." Vee rocked back and forth, emitting soft groans. "I puke everywhere. We're talking projectile. Even my stepbrothers get grossed out." She belched loudly.

Where had Vee learned *that?* Esther pressed her lips together. She didn't want to give Vee away.

"I'm cold and wet, and this truck smells——"

It did smell. Like old wet animal something.

Whispering so hard in Esther's ear that Esther shoved a shoulder up to protect her hearing, Sunny said, "When he stops for Vee, pull up the lock and fall out."

Why me? Esther twitched a look out at the gloomy woods, the muddy road pitted with puddles. Falling out would hurt. But then, being kidnapped wasn't living the yayness.

Leaning forward between the seats, Aneta sneezed violently and wetly. "Ah'b catching a code." She leaned back against Vee. "Ah'b gedding sick."

The masked man shuddered and pulled up the hood on his raincoat, slowing down for another puddle. Steering with one hand, he opened a cell phone and punched a number with his thumb.

"You'd better meet me at the house. You have to help me take care of something."

They *had* to hurry. He was calling his accomplice. Every criminal had an accomplice.

It helped that Aneta was in the game now. She *never* sneezed juicily. Aneta's sneezes were dainty little "ah-choos." Come to think of it, she'd never been sick.

He drove on. Vee belched and retched, and Aneta sneezed and coughed. Still he drove.

Drastic measures. It was something her mother said when they were trying to get Siddy to stop repeating phrases.

The right front wheel of the truck slipped off the edge of a hole, and everyone fell toward the right again. Esther reached over Sunny, jerked up the lock, shoved open the door, and rolled over her friend out the door. Sunny leaped behind her and hit her behind the knees.

"Ow!" Esther yelped, momentarily pinned by the sturdy Sunny. In a flash, Sunny was off her and pulling her up.

"Run! *Run!*"

The two girls pelted down the muddy road toward the gate. Looking back, they saw the brake lights of the truck blaze on, and then *it kept going*.

"This is Big Trouble." Sunny moved to a sprint. "He's so evil he wouldn't stop. We have to get help."

"Our bikes are under the tree!" Esther panted, trying to keep up with Sunny who played soccer with C.P., an eleven-year-old boy who lived across the fence from Aneta and was a good friend of the S.A.V.E. Squad. Esther avoided running. In fact, the only time she ran was when she was with the S.A.V.E. Squad. "We'll go to Uncle Dave's."

"I—I. . ." Even Sunny was puffing in the rain. She skidded momentarily on a slippery spot in the road and waved her arms wildly to keep her balance. "There's a farm before Uncle Dave's. On this side of the road. I've seen it before."

Even closer help. Good.

The gate loomed in the gray light. Now that it was getting closer to late afternoon than early afternoon, the gloom had increased.

"Oh, hurry!" Esther panted. What if her legs wouldn't pedal when they got to the bikes? What if the fence had locked behind the truck? What if Vee and Aneta tried to save themselves and the wounded owls and Masked Man—? She wouldn't go there. She and Sunny would save the day.

They reached the gate at the same moment a Volkswagen Bug, windshield wipers slapping furiously, turned off the county road and pulled in front of the gate. The headlights speared the girls into paralysis.

Was this help or worse—Big Trouble?

"Do we run?" Sunny looked miserable with her coat gleaming in the headlights. "It's all woods. We could get lost and *never* get help for Vee and Aneta."

Esther thought about all the books she'd read about kids who beat the bad guys. "Well, there's two of us. One of—"

The door opened, and a tall, skinny figure swathed in an orange fluorescent poncho stepped out. "Sunny? Is that you?"

It was the Bird Lady from the community center! Esther looked at Sunny, eyes wide. It had gotten worse. The Bird Lady was in cahoots with Masked Man.

"What do we do, what do we do?" Sunny wasn't asking a question. She was simply panicking, and Esther joined her. If they ran, the car could run them down. If they stayed to fight, they might have a better chance.

There was only one problem.

Esther had never fought anybody. Sure, she'd wrestled with her brothers, but that was never life and death. She was pretty sure Sunny hadn't beaten anyone up either.

The woman fished under the poncho and withdrew something that she pointed at them. The girls hit the mud face-first. Immediately, the gate began to creak open.

Chapter 5

Meeting Bird Man

$\mathcal{B}$ut he said you two had to 'take care of something,' and in the movies that always means bad stuff for the heroes." Esther pulled off her soaking coat in the now-steamy Bug. In the backseat, Sunny leaned forward, resting her arms on the two front seats so she wouldn't miss a word.

Bird Lady's thin shoulders shook, and her voice held a tremble. "He meant he had injured birds to care for. That's what Byron always says when he calls me. He tries to stay very calm, even though he's worried for the birds." She steered slowly around a full puddle smack in the middle of the driveway. They were headed to, it turned out, her twin *brother's* house. "But he didn't have time to say that he also had four girls who had taken over the truck and were threatening him."

"We didn't threaten him." Esther felt it important to be accurate here.

"Apparently one of you said that your mother was a solicitor—or what you Americans call a lawyer—and that he'd better let them go."

The two girls smiled big. "That's our Aneta."

"My brother was quite concerned that one of you would chunder all over him from the backseat. He said the impending doom was quite terrifying."

The two were silent for a breath, then Esther said, "Is *chunder* British for puke?"

Bird Lady nodded.

"That's our Vee! She was good. I thought she really would yak," Sunny put in. "We only would have hurt him if he'd started hurting the birds."

"Or us," Esther agreed.

The shoulders shook again. "You girls must be very good friends with very good imaginations."

"The Squaders are my best friends on the planet," Esther said. Shivers shook her from deep inside. It had been pretty scary when the gate creaked open until Bird Lady's voice bellowed out Esther's name. Even then, it took Sunny and Esther a few minutes in the mud before the woman convinced them that Vee and Aneta were safe and the man with the mask was Bird Lady's brother, Byron Beake, who was actually a hero. Esther didn't get all of it since Bird Lady was speaking so quickly with her British accent, but it had something to do with animals and a fire and Byron being a hero. The mask had something to do with his face being burned.

Moments later, they made a final turn on the driveway, which had turned to muddy mush, and there it was. Not just a house. Tall, three stories, with a big porch and a rounded left side. A couple of shutters sagged crazily away from windows. Paint peeled off the area around the door. Lights glowed inside, yet it still looked like a place that would have a creepy butler.

"Wow." Sunny leaned forward to get a better look. "That looks like some house in a scary movie."

Beverly Beake put the Bug in PARK, nodding. "Byron has a lot to do to fix it up. But he likes it because it's—" She hesitated and then shook her head. "No matter. Let's go see these wee owls."

Shooting a glance at each other, Sunny and Esther trooped in behind Beverly, Esther sniggering to herself that they were following the *Bird* Lady, Beverly *Beake*. It seemed easier to call her Bird Lady than Beverly. At the extra-tall front door, Bird Lady turned the doorknob, the head of a snarling lion. She pushed open the heavy door.

Inside was a wide foyer with a room off to the left and firelight coming from the right. *What a place*, thought Esther as she and Sunny ran to meet Vee and Aneta who leaped up from enormous wing chairs by a fireplace that looked big enough to sleep in. The fire was piled high with large logs, sending out welcome heat. Esther couldn't wait to stand in front of it. The chills were twitching her shoulders all by themselves.

Byron Beake, standing by the fire, muttered something that sounded like "hullo."

"You're here!" Aneta threw her arms around Sunny, squeezed her, and then did the same to Esther. "You are safe. We are safe. Mr. Beake says the owls need lots of help. He put them in his bird hospital."

He had a bird hospital? She regarded the tall, spare man standing in the shadows at the edge of the fireplace, arms folded. He wasn't smiling. Beverly laid her wet coat over a chair near the fire and watched her brother on the other side. She was smiling, like she knew a secret he didn't.

So they had actually jumped in the truck of someone who could help? Another great S.A.V.E. Squad rescue. They *were* good. Living the yayness, as Sunny would say.

"Uncle Dave knows we're here now, and he says, well—I guess we kind of got it wrong about Mr. *Beake*." Vee was trying not to laugh.

"We're not in danger."

Esther couldn't blame her. *I mean really. . .Beake?* Were Vee and Aneta wondering about the mask? How could they not be?

"Now that we're here, what do we do to help the owls?" She'd made it to the fireplace. Oh, it was toasty. She wondered briefly if Mr. Beake had supplies for s'mores.

The Bird Man's long nose twitched as his lip curled.

"Byron." Beverly's voice held a warning. She moved to stand next to Esther by the fire. "I've heard about these girls in town. They—"

"They aren't getting within ten miles of my owls." While the girls filled each other in, he hadn't said a word; now this single sentence was icy clear.

"*Your* owls?" Vee's dark brows slammed together. . .the look Aneta had dubbed the Vee Stare gathering on her face.

"But. . ." Aneta's voice trailed off. She looked at the other girls, her expression asking, *Did I hear what I think I heard?*

His owls? Those two bitty owls were *their* owls. Esther frowned and placed her hands on her hips. Before she could correct him, however, Byron had risen and was moving toward a door at the back of the room.

"Take them home, Beverly," he said, tossing the words over his shoulder. When Vee began to speak, he spun around and stabbed a long, bony finger at each girl, punctuating his words. "Don't. Ever. Come. Back."

Chapter 6

Something's Up

I know you're going to say life's not fair, Dad, but it was really *really* not fair that Masked Man kicked us out and we had to leave those hurt baby owls with him!" Anger choked Esther's throat so she couldn't swallow the mouthful of chicken rice casserole. As soon as she'd gotten home, her mother made her take a long hot shower and pull on fleece pj's. No more shivering.

Her father, who called himself "Mr. Medium with a Big God," regarded her with his medium brown eyes. They matched his medium brown hair. Taking another forkful of the peas that accompanied the casserole, a smile hovered over his lips before he inserted what Toby called "the usual" Saturday dinner.

"Now how did you know I would say that?" he murmured to no one in particular.

"Because you always do!" Esther and Toby chorused.

All eyes were on him—Esther's mom, whose eyes looked more tired than usual, Toby, Esther's younger brother by two years, and Sidney, the youngest at just over three.

"Masked Man!" Sidney shouted, and Esther sighed. She never

should have called Mr. Beake that. Now Sidney would shout "Masked Man" for days until another phrase caught his attention. It would be majorly embarrassing if Byron Beake ever heard it. Of course, "Byron Beake" might set Siddy off as well. Sidney loved sounds, although at more than three years old, he didn't talk correctly. Mom and Dad had been taking him to a lot of doctors the last few months. Esther had noted more than one set of looks traded back and forth between them when Siddy shouted the same thing endlessly. Never in a whisper. Ever.

"Dad! We need to help the owls. We found them." Maybe if she raised her voice like Sidney, they would listen to her.

"Esther!" Her mother's voice cut sharply into Esther's volume.

Her face flushing, she shot a glance at her father and muttered, "Sorry for yelling, Dad."

He winked at her.

"Why do you call him Masked Man?" Toby, who always finished first, was done. He reached for the last spoonful of chicken, rice, and chicken soup. His mom slapped his hand away.

"Not until your father's done."

Always that. It didn't matter how hungry they were, Mom never let them have seconds until Dad had what he wanted. Usually there wasn't enough to go around a full second time. Toby and Esther ate a lot of bread with peanut butter and honey right after dinner.

"We never even got to ask him how he was going to help them." Important questions like, "What animals have you helped before?" Mr. Beake had simply told them to never come back and left the room. Miss Beake had sighed and, looking like a sad turkey buzzard wearing a poncho, herded the girls back into the Bug and driven them to Uncle Dave's. There, phone calls with parents followed, and the S.A.V.E. Squad girls found themselves each back at home with no sleepover and lots of questions from parents. "He sure was grouchy."

"Masked Man!" Sidney shouted, attempting to stand in his booster seat set in the dining room chair.

"Down boy," Esther's dad said, patting the seat. "Cheeks in the seat, please."

"Cheeks in the seat!" Sidney bellowed.

Esther's mom sighed and picked at her dinner.

"Does it look like a robber mask?" Toby persisted.

"No." She frowned, trying to describe it. "It was clear and, like, squished right against his face." Now that she thought about it—now that she wasn't sopping wet and her teeth weren't chattering—parts of his scalp held only wispy hairs. No wonder he'd looked like a monster when he looked in the window. It had been the mask she'd seen and not him pressing his face against the window. *He wasn't trying to scare us.*

Esther's mom nodded. "A burn mask." She looked at her husband. "I've seen people wearing those when we do hospital visits." Her eyes filled with tears. "I love those visits."

"Jessica." Dad's voice was gentle.

What was *with* everyone tonight? She and the girls had nearly been killed by the storm, kidnapped, and had their owls stolen. Nobody seemed to care. Now, if it had been *Sidney* in trouble. . . *Trouble* reminded her that she hadn't told the Squad the Melissa news.

Toby and Esther fell quiet. Although Toby could be a spectacular pain sometimes, Esther knew he was a softie about people being hurt.

"Cheeks in the seat!" Sidney shouted.

Esther sighed. She bet the S.A.V.E. Squad girls never had meals like the Martins.

Chapter 7

No More Rescues?

On Monday, the first day of Spring Break, Nadine, the Squad's friend and children's librarian, swiveled in her big leather chair to face the four girls who sprawled behind the oversized wooden desk. It was a Squad thing to do, Esther thought, rolling over onto her stomach and dropping her head onto her two fists. Meet with Nadine at the library. Solve a mystery. Get ideas. It was kind of like their clubhouse. Especially when they were fresh out of ideas. Maybe whatever was puttering around at the back of Esther's mind would come out and say, "Hey!" Like something she was supposed to tell the girls.

"I don't think I've ever heard you four be so quiet. What's up?" Nadine pushed long, dark bangs out of her eyes.

"Not *what* so much as a 'whooooooo' from Beake Man." Sunny let out a snort and then explained the whole sorry owl mess to Nadine. "He hasn't called any of us back."

Nadine nodded, her head tipped to the side. "Hmm. I know Beverly a little. She's been coming to the Arts Council meetings." The library, the senior center, and the community center all shared different sides of the big community center building by the lake.

"She's quite a bird expert. So is her brother."

"Byron Beake." Vee sniffed when Sunny let out another snort. "Can you believe that's his real name?"

Esther hoped Sidney never heard it. She had been pretty careful keeping the Squad away from her house, giving one excuse after another why they should meet at Aneta's (". . .but we can swim and play with Wink!"), or Vee's (". . .but your little kitty is so much fun to play with"), or Sunny's Uncle Dave's ranch (". . .but the animals! We can play with the animals!"). There'd be no telling what Sidney would think he'd heard and then start yelling. It wasn't that she didn't love her little brother, she simply didn't know how to *explain* him.

Sunny, never one to sit still for long, shifted to her back and began to pedal her legs in the air. "My parents said it was better that we didn't get attached to the owls like we always do to the animals we save."

With a familiar move, Vee pulled the small notebook out of her back jeans pocket. "My mom and stepmom both said they'd heard about the Beakes"—another chortle from Sunny and a smothered one from Aneta—"and that Byron is like an important person in the bird world. He has a license to help wild raptors." She fished around her hair band that held back the shiny hair and pulled out the tiny pen. She began to doodle.

Aneta chimed in with her story that Sunny's Uncle Dave said he'd met Byron soon after he'd moved in. "He likes him. He says he's different, but in a good way."

"Different, but in a good way," Esther repeated under her breath. Hmm.

"So we do not have a rescue anymore. That was much faster than the last one." Aneta looked like she regretted it.

"Well, I guess we go back to our other projects." Esther knew they had to do something to help animals. It wasn't like the Squad to sit around.

"You girls did such a good job with your projects that other people now want to help." Nadine swung back around and began sifting through books, checking each one off on a list in front of her.

"What?" A general cry sprang from four outraged throats.

Nadine ticked off each project on three fingers as she explained. The pickleball ladies and the senior center wanted to do the Basset Waddle in August. Two older citizens the girls had befriended were working with the community cats after the girls had completed their Great Cat Caper.

"That brings us to Major the mini horse and the zoo." Sunny stopped pedaling and let her legs flop to the floor. "Whew! My family does that as a family outreach."

A long silence followed Sunny's statement. Esther felt a little sad. No rescues.

Then Aneta spoke up. "I have an idea." She unfolded her long legs and stood, stretching her arms over her head—first one side then the other.

Esther waited on her stomach, waving her legs, holding her head in her fists. When Aneta didn't continue, Esther flopped to the side and peered up at her taller friend.

Aneta had frozen like a statue in a park, arms still high. Her mouth hung open, and then, ever so slowly as though the statue were melting, she pointed. Esther scrambled to her feet, following the finger. Vee and Sunny were standing as well.

Their blond friend's mouth closed then opened, trying to form words. "*Melissa!*" It was a single word of panic.

Oh. *That's* what Esther had forgotten to tell the girls. As Aneta collapsed behind Nadine's desk, Esther filled them in with Melissa news.

"So what's her unfortunate accident?" Vee watched Melissa direct C.P. as he steered a loaded book cart. "Must be her hands. C.P. is pushing the cart."

"I bet she told C.P. that she had to do the important work of putting the books back on the shelf." Sunny turned to Esther. "Is she coming back to Aneta's school after break?"

A whimper floated up from the floor. "Nooooooo!"

Sunny reached down and patted Aneta on the head.

Esther lifted her shoulders in a shrug. Melissa, C.P., and the cart disappeared, and moments later C.P. scared the daylights out of them, appearing from behind in the stacks and whispering, "Yah!"

"No fair, C.P." Vee shot him the Vee Stare. "So what accident is Melissa recovering from?"

C.P. didn't know and didn't care. He only cared that he got roped into being Melissa's servant with the cart, and now he was hiding. "I get to go to my aunt's for Spring Break tomorrow, so I only have to hide for the rest of today."

"That bunch of girls doesn't hang out with her now that she's back," Esther observed. "Usually they are everywhere she is." She remembered what Melissa had said about the S.A.V.E. Squad. "You guys, she told me she was moving on from those girls because things change. I told her the Squad didn't change." Licking her lips nervously at the memory, she repeated Melissa's words.

"Nothing to worry about." Vee lifted one shoulder in dismissal. "Nothing is going to change the S.A.V.E. Squad."

"Can't happen." Sunny walked to the end of the aisle on her toes and then skipped back.

Aneta uttered another moan.

Esther felt better. No change. Just the way she liked it.

Now they needed to focus on helping those hurt owls, even if Beake Man thought they were trouble.

Chapter 8

Everything Changes

That evening Esther snuggled into the floral swing cushions next to her dad. Her mom leaned against him on the other side. "When I saw the smaller owl, his big round eyes looked up at me, and they were so scared. At least I think they looked scared. Birds can get scared like humans, can't they?" With her ear pressed to his side, she could hear her dad's heart thump-thumping.

Her dad said, "Mmm."

Right foot tucked under, her mother pushed the swing with her other foot.

Creak, creak crunched the chain in the wood roof over the deck. Toby and Siddy were inside watching TV. The rain pattered gently with no wind to get them wet on the back deck. Esther breathed in the fresh dirt smell, liking it.

Maybe she should give up thinking about the owls. Esther slid a little bit farther down. Dad was such a nice leaning post. She thought of those two little-ish birds with the Beake Man. After all, he had training and a license to help wild birds.

Creak, creak. A sigh from her mother.

Esther's thoughts ran along. He might know how to take care of them, but would he love them like the Squad would? Could you love wild things? Perhaps Beake Man would change his mind when he learned what the S.A.V.E. Squad was all about. Really. *There isn't anything like the Squad.*

"I'm so glad I'm part of the S.A.V.E. Squad," she said, her voice slipping into sleepy. She was so tired. "I want us to be the Squad forever."

Nudging her, her dad said in his medium voice, "Stay awake, kiddo. Mom and I need to talk with you, since you're the oldest."

All the warm, comfy feelings vanished as though spring had *poofed!* and the cold winds of winter had returned to blast through the back deck. *Since you're the oldest* had been what her parents had said when her grandmother had died. They had told her first. *Since you're the oldest*, the year the long-awaited vacation in Hawaii fell through.

After the first words, she was aware her dad talked on. However, only certain phrases stabbed through the suffocating haze of *oh no*. Words and phrases like: "Meet new friends," "Know this is hard," "Best for getting help for Siddy. . ." She couldn't speak, couldn't move. The icy fingers of dread had clutched her heart and flash frozen it as what Dad was *not* saying hit her.

When her family moved at the end of the school year, she, Esther Martin, *would not be a S.A.V.E. Squad girl.* A hard knot of ick curled inside her along with a pinching of bitterness. It wasn't fair.

Gradually, her brain cleared enough for her to decide that since her life would be over when she moved at the end of the school year, the Squad had to finish one final brilliant project.

The owls.

Chapter 9

Talking Crazy

Should I tell them? Should I not tell them? Clutching her terrible secret and coming in dead last, Esther climbed off her mountain bike at the black-iron gate the next day and collapsed, gasping. "Guys—*gasp*—was it necessary to race *all* the way from the library?" She lay on the semidry leaves and gravel and heard the girls giggle.

Aneta carefully set down her bike and pulled off her helmet. "Esther, we still had fun coming in last."

"No, you still were ahead of me. I was last last," Esther called from her prone position.

"My dad says the more you move your molecules, the better your brain solves problems," Vee said. She and Sunny had been wheel to wheel right until the black-iron fence began at the Beakes' property, when sturdy Sunny groaned and pumped two quick pedals to pull ahead.

If Vee's dad was right, Esther thought, making herself breathe slowly, but not so slowly that she passed out, she would be a genius by the time they rode home. She'd moved her molecules more with the Squad than she'd ever done in her life. The Squad never walked, they ran; and they never coasted, they pedaled. Hard. Fortunately, her plan to get the Beake Man to let them see the owls involved no running or jumping. It was all in the brain.

It had to work. School would be out the second week of June and then, well, and then everything would fall apart. The owls *must* be their final, best rescue.

"Esther, this is the craziest plan ever. I don't think it's going to work." Off her bike and without her helmet, Vee eyed Esther with a doubtful expression. "It's just plain—weird."

In their previous adventures, she and Vee had often butted heads because they both thought they were the smartest girls in the Squad. If any of the girls were going to get into a bossy party, it was her and Vee. Vee thought all her ideas were great. Well, Esther had some great ideas, too.

Since this was the last mission, the plan *needed* to be crazy enough to work. Already, Esther was watching for "the last this" and "the last that." Maybe this was the last time she and Vee would disagree? *Right.* She awkwardly struggled to her feet. On to the plan.

The four girls lined up, side by side, and faced the looming black fence. Esther handed out their parts. Vee pursed her lips. "I think we should agree that if he lets us in, fine. If he doesn't. . ." Her voice trailed off.

"No!" Esther said it more loudly than she had intended. She had actually shouted it. "We must get in. It's—" She searched for the biggest word she knew and found nothing. "Important."

Sunny, Aneta, and Vee looked startled.

"Well, okaaaaay." Vee's mouth turned down.

Should she tell them right now that this was their last project? What if they felt sorry for her and went along? No, they had to do it because it was the right thing to do, a Squad thing to do—get in there and help the owls.

"Because he's British, we're going to show him we speak British. Then he'll see we're okay." She stepped to the intercom and pushed the button. "Hello? Mr. Beake?"

An electronic squeal that preceded the rough and scratchy accented growl of Byron Beake made the girls jump. "I told you to never come back! Take your bikes and go!"

The girls looked around. Esther frowned. How did he know they were riding bikes?

Sunny bounced forward and punched the buttons. "Whoa, how did you know it was us and that we're riding bikes?"

The metallic voice rasped, "Because I am watching you on a security camera. Now. Go. Away."

Desperately, Esther stuck her mouth near the intercom, pushed the button, and read from her piece of paper. In her very best, newly practiced *British accent*.

"Ay-up, Mr. Beake!" She stepped away from the intercom and nodded to Aneta, who hurried forward.

"You might 'ave got a blinkered view, guv—"

Aneta's British accent was better than hers, Esther thought approvingly. Aneta rolled her eyes and gave way to Sunny who had to press her lips together tightly to stop the laughter.

"—'bout wot we want to do," Sunny said in the worst British accent Esther had ever heard.

Now it was Vee's turn. She took a deep breath, plugged her nose, and read, "So wot do you say, me bright lad?" Stepping away, she tipped her head at the sky as if to say, "I can't believe I just did that."

Nothing.

The girls waited.

Answer, pleaded Esther silently. If she knew how to climb a fence and actually liked climbing a fence—neither of which she did—and if she could sprint, which she couldn't—she'd leap over and race toward the house. The Squad *had* to complete their last mission together. Before she had to move.

Esther thought they were very patient, but the rasping, metallic voice didn't return.

"He hates us," Vee said.

Aneta nodded her head.

"How could he hate us?" Sunny sounded so puzzled the others laughed.

"I know. We are so cool. We have a history of helping animals. He must not know that." Esther frowned.

A high-pitched buzz signaled a reply.

"Hi, girls. It's Beverly. Loved your accents. My brother is opening the gate. C'mon in. Byron was"—a pause—"very touched by your trying to make him feel comfortable."

The gate began to swing inward. Victory! The girls slapped their hands together up high, Squad bracelets on each arm. Walking in a straight line along the muddy road, the girls wondered aloud about what made him change his mind.

"I think his sister told him to be nice. That's what Dad is always telling me. Be nice to the Twin Terrors." Vee's stepbrothers adored her. She was getting better about liking them but was a long way from adoring yet. She told the girls it was tough getting past them touching all her stuff when she stayed with them for Dad Weekends.

Sunny ran ahead to spin in circles, head tipped back. "I love this road. Guys, when you tip your head back and spin, you can see—" A giant stagger, and she was bottom down in a mud puddle. "Ouch!"

The girls raced to help her up. Now wet from the waistband of her jeans and dripping into her hikers, Sunny made a face. "Well, I guess

I can't recommend that move."

In a few more moments, with Sunny walking "like a duck" as Vee said, they pushed open a low, creaking black-iron gate to the house and bounced up the stairs. Esther stepped forward and thudded the grumpy-looking gargoyle door knocker.

Slowly the door creaked open. Byron Beake stood in the doorway, the mask making his expression difficult to read. Was that a smile? The mask mushed out his lips. And was it a nice smile or an evil smile? She was glad Bird Lady was there.

Maybe it was a good thing they couldn't read his face as he opened the door farther to admit them into the gloomy foyer without a word. She had a strong feeling "sister power" had made him open the gate. She made her brothers do stuff they didn't want to do all the time. Well. Not all the time. Wouldn't it be great if they did? She resolved to work harder on that. Especially with Siddy. It was hard to get Siddy to do anything he didn't want to do.

Thinking of her brother reminded her of Sunny saying that Uncle Dave said Byron Beake was different, and that wasn't a bad thing. Maybe for him. She didn't like being different. Being different meant she couldn't bring the Squad to her house, and it meant that Melissa had a lot of things she could criticize her about. A bit of worry crossed her thoughts. The girls hadn't seemed to notice that Melissa was talking about *her* joining *their* Squad. Esther was quite clear on that. She shook her head and shoved her hand in her pocket, feeling the reassuring crackle of paper. The Beake Man had to let them help. It was the last time the Squad would be together on a mission. Her eyes began to sting. She blinked quickly.

Byron moved to the fireplace, once again roaring against the damp cold of spring. Propping himself against the mantel, he simply watched the girls, his face aglow in the light. The fireplace felt wonderful. Its warmth reached out to Esther, and she wondered if where they were moving had rainy springs and mud puddles.

"So you want to help." He made it sound like they wanted to burn down his house.

"Yes." Vee stood in front of him, her hand furiously motioning Esther to do the same. Trust Vee to want to take over. The tight spot in Esther that began the night on the swing clutched.

Esther pulled the paper from her pocket and handed it to Byron. "This is our résumé of how we've helped other animals."

"We love animals," Aneta added.

"We love to help!" Sunny got halfway round in a spin until she caught Byron's glare. "Oh. Sorry."

"We have Frank and Nadine for references if you need them. Miss Beake knows Nadine."

Beverly Beake entered the room carrying a silver tray with teacups and what Esther knew the British called biscuits, which were really cookies, and nodded. "I work with both of them with my bird education classes. They think the world of these girls."

Sunny muttered, "Well, maybe not Frank."

Aneta shoved an elbow into her friend's ribs. Sunny yelped and leaped away, banging into a low side table with a shepherdess figurine. The table began to tip, and Sunny windmilled her arms. "Guys!"

Byron made a leap toward the table, but Vee's long legs were already there, one hand on the table and one carefully holding the figurine in place.

"No problem," she said nonchalantly. "So what do you think of our qualifications?"

At this use of *qualifications*, a slow smile oozed across his face. Mask or no mask, Esther didn't like the looks of it.

Chapter 10

Beake Man Is Up to Something

If you want to help with the two owls, you have to pass a test." He rocked back on his heels.

"Byron." His sister's voice held a warning. He ignored her, stretching out a hand to the four who had retreated to their tight bunch. "Come on, I'll show you the place. And how you can help the owls."

They passed through the door back into the foyer and headed deeper into the house. They peeked in at a large kitchen on the right and a sunny room on the left. As they stepped out the back door, a low screech that sounded like a billion scraping metal nails on a metal auditorium seat smacked their ears.

The girls dropped to a crouch.

"We heard that from the road!" Sunny gasped, looking up at Beake Man with wide eyes.

"So you want to help birds, do you?" Beake Man said, the first chuckle bubbling out of his throat. "Well, the first thing to learn is that they are not pets, like those other animals you helped. They eat those animals. These are birds of prey."

"What was that screech?" Vee stood and brushed off the leaves and mud from the knees of her jeans, grimacing.

"Sounded like a monster." Aneta rose.

Esther scrambled to her feet as well. How could Aneta, tall, blond, and beautiful, not have her tan pants get dirty after dropping on the ground? Esther glanced down at her right leg where a long, brown, wet stripe was soaking into her leg. So not fair.

"It's a peregrine falcon. He's seen me and is saying hello."

"You said they couldn't be pets." Vee's chin rose a bit.

"He wasn't born to be a pet. Let's say we have a *tenuous* relationship. I feed him, and he lets me train him. Most of the time anyway."

"How come he's here? We want the owls to go back to being owls, not stay in a cage."

"Ah, yes. The idealism of the young." Byron folded his arms and regarded the girls. "People are most of the problem for why these birds can't go back to the wild. These birds get shot, hit by cars, caught in horrible antibird sprays. They live, but they can no longer function in the wild. They would—" He paused, stroking the fine, sparse hairs on his head.

"—be toast," Sunny supplied with a bob of her head.

Byron pointed to a large cage with tree stumps, bushes, and perches in it. "This is Howard's pen." A strange black, white, and red bird hustled around inside. A turkey buzzard. Esther recognized again the similarity between Beverly Beake and this bird. Standing next to the screened wall, he darted his head at Esther's feet. She backed away.

"What's he doing?"

"Shoelaces," Byron said. "He was found injured a few years ago. Was hit by a car while eating roadkill. Another group rehabbed him, but the bird imprinted on humans and when they set him free, he became a pest at the local park, swooping from the sky to picnickers' shoelaces. Tended to scare people. So he ended up here. When it's just him and me, he follows me around."

Another look at Howard. Esther didn't think she'd like to have a picnic where he swooped either. Esther was beginning to wonder if letting Beake Man take care of their owls was a good thing. Maybe he liked that they stayed with him. The girls wanted them to be able to fly off and be wild.

Beake Man pointed out the peregrine falcon's flight cage, where the bird could actually swoop around. "I take him out to train him." No sign of the bird.

"Where is he?" Esther asked. Beake Man said he was hiding in the foliage.

"What's his story?" Aneta asked.

Lifting one shoulder as though the question weren't important, Byron continued walking toward another building.

"Bill would love that garage," Vee said, increasing her pace. "It's huge!"

Tall and white with black-iron latches on rolling doors that slid left and right to open, it reminded Esther of the carriage houses in the public television shows her family watched. Fancy and plain carriages stayed in carriage houses until the groom was instructed to bring one or another out for the rich people. She couldn't wait to see inside.

Beake Man slid the towering door to the right, wheels rumbling.

Eagerly, the girls hustled in after Byron, blinking their eyes to adjust to the semidarkness. As Byron flipped a switch near the door, the interior brightened. Before them were covered, tall, upright rectangles. A refrigerator, a steel table, and a large two-section sink stood on the left wall. Byron had quietly passed three rectangles, and as he passed, one let out a squawk.

The girls traded looks. Birds in those cages!

"So girls, tell me what you do know about raptors," Beake Man said over his shoulder, having reached the steel table and leaned upon it to face them. Again that smile.

"I don't like his smile," Esther hissed to Vee. "Why was he so mean to us and kicked us out and now he's showing us around?"

"Isn't that what you wanted?" Vee's dark brows slammed together. "I don't get you sometimes, Esther."

That hurt. Especially when the Squad was on their last mission together. If she'd told the girls she had to move, would Vee have said that? Or was that how Vee really felt about her? Her stomach began to hurt.

"But see? I was right we'd need to know about owls and stuff." She'd done her research.

Vee grunted.

The pinch of bitterness nipped. Hunching her shoulders, she increased her pace to catch up with Aneta, who smiled at her. In front of them, and just behind Beake Man, Sunny repeated the information Esther had passed on to the Squad. "We know they are called raptors—"

"And are birds of prey." Aneta recited what she'd memorized from her paper Esther provided the girls.

"Owl pellets, which is their—" Vee hesitated.

"You can say 'poop,' Vee. It's their poop, and if you cut it open, you can see what they ate." Sunny bounced on her toes.

Leave it to Sunny to just spit it all out. Esther frowned then told herself to stop being grumpy. Their plan had been to make sure Beake Man knew they weren't just stupid kids.

Whatever his tests were, they *had* to pass them.

"Oh, good to know," Beake Man said.

Esther narrowed her eyes. Were his shoulders shaking like his sister's did when she was silently laughing?

Pointing to one of the cages, he said, "The two juveniles you found are in here because it's quiet." He spun around so he was facing the girls. "*Quiet.*"

The four nodded. Esther thought about letting him know nicely that they weren't kindergarten babies. Scared animals needed quiet. They learned that with the community cats. *Sheesh.*

Beake Man moved to one of the tall beams supporting the building and flipped another switch. The rest of the interior brightened like sunrise. Not too bright. It was kind of cool. That wouldn't scare the owls like the fluorescent lights at school. Those lights made her eyes tired sometimes.

A tall cage, completely shrouded in canvas tarp, stood off to the left.

He gestured. "Here they are."

The girls waited. When he made no move to take off the canvas walls hiding the owls, Sunny bounced and said, "Aren't you going to take off the canvas thingies?"

He shoved his hands in his pockets. "No."

Sunny looked at Vee. Vee looked at Aneta. Aneta looked at Esther. *What?*

Vee was chewing on the inside of her bottom lip. "Why not?"

"I want to see how they're doing. Are they okay? Did the one owl stop bleeding? Was the other one hurt badly?" Sunny was still hopping up and down.

Beake Man finally looked happy, which Esther couldn't figure out. At. All.

"Because wild birds being around people isn't good for them. They need to not trust people. People hurt them." The look he gave them was one that shouted, PEOPLE LIKE YOU KIDS.

"But we didn't hurt them," Aneta said. "We helped them. Can't we just see them?"

"No."

Esther straightened up from her slump. "So if nobody is supposed to see them, how come you can see them?"

"I used gloves to clean the wounds."

"Are they okay?" Sunny stopped bouncing.

Beake Man told the girls that it would be touch and go for the smaller owl. The other owl hadn't been shot, but there was something wrong with one of his wings that Beake Man had yet to figure out.

"And how do you feed them if you're not supposed to see them?" Vee was giving him the Vee Stare. If anything bugged Vee, it was being told she couldn't do something and then knowing someone else had.

He jerked a hand to another covered table. "I feed them with a robotic arm, watch through a camera, and use an owl puppet to simulate the mother owl."

"A puppet!" Aneta smiled for the first time since Byron had ignored her question.

So there was no way to help. Esther's heart clutched. No last mission for the S.A.V.E. Squad. The weeks would go by, everyone would get busy, and the Squad would never be together. She would leave and that would be that.

"Unless," Beake Man said, looking up at the open rafters where smaller birds could be seen flitting around their nests. "You could help in a different way."

"We'll do it!" Vee pounced on the possibility.

Sunny spun, remembered, hunched her shoulders, and stopped. "Yayness!" she whispered.

Aneta beamed.

Esther blew out a big breath. That had been a close call. The knot in her stomach loosened. "Sure. We can help. What do you want us to do?"

Beake Man led them over to the kitchen. "Stand here." He pointed to the long, stainless-steel counter. The girls walked over and stood obediently. Esther wondered what was in the drawers below the counter. Probably bowls and spoons?

Beake Man eyed them for a moment, like he was going to say something, then he shrugged and turned away to the fridge. He took out a large plastic container with a red lid like Esther's mom used after she made a lot of pea soup. She recognized it because she hated pea soup and groaned inside when she saw the container come out. It meant a lot of days of pea soup for lunch and pea soup for snacks.

Beake Man placed the container on the counter. "You have to prepare what they would eat in the wild. Since they can't fly yet, they can't catch their food."

Pulling the lid off the container, he pushed the bottom toward the girls and continued, "Cut each one in half, and then I'll show you how the robotic arm works."

Four heads leaned over the container and then jerked back.

"But, but—," Aneta said, backing away.

"It's—" Sunny gulped.

"They're dead mice!" Esther's voice sounded like it was squeezing out of a tiny space.

So that's why he was smiling. Sure they could help the owls. With cutting up dead mice.

The big door rolled open, and everyone turned to look. Outlined with the brightness outside, the silhouette stood small in the doorway, but the tilt of the head and a toss of the hair told Esther helping the owls was about to get worse.

"Ms. Beake told me I could find you all here. I hope I haven't come too late to help."

Aneta's gasp was loud enough to echo off the wide beams.

Chapter 11

Epic Fail

Melissa stepped through the doorway, made her way to Beake Man, and extended her hand. "Thank you so much for allowing me to help you here with your amazing service to animals."

Beake Man just stood there. Esther was sure the word was "goggling." He stood there goggling at Melissa's big speech.

What was going on? How did Melissa get in? A quick peek at S.A.V.E. Squad faces told Esther they were wondering the same thing.

"How did you get in?" Vee sounded like she did the very first time Sunny, Vee, Aneta, and Esther had ever seen each other. The very unfriendly voice Vee was so very good at.

"Oh, my dad called his friend the mayor to see what type of volunteering I could do while I'm"—*did she hesitate the tiniest bit?*—"recovering from my accident."

Vee muttered an ugly sound, Sunny said "hunh," and Aneta didn't say anything.

The mayor, thought Esther as Melissa pushed past her. The mayor thought the S.A.V.E. Squad a fine example to the city and its children. Esther sighed. But the mayor also thought all kids got along as long as they were kept busy on "worthy service projects."

The S.A.V.E. Squad could have told her that didn't happen.

Now Melissa had busted herself into a S.A.V.E. Squad rescue. Anybody who'd ever talked to the rich girl for more than two minutes knew Melissa didn't care about anything but herself. She was up to something. She'd been mad at the Squad since their first adventure.

Esther would be watching *very carefully.*

"Oh, for the love of mud." Beake Man shook his head and stopped goggling. Rummaging in a drawer below the counter in front of him, he pulled out five knives. Esther's stomach pitched a half flip and hung there. *Uh-oh.* That halfway stomach flip usually meant she was going to throw up. Unless she distracted herself.

"Cut the mice in half and put the pieces in this bowl." He produced a medium-sized silver bowl from another larger drawer.

Sunny and Vee were shooting side looks at each other. They were closest to the counter with Esther behind them. Aneta was behind Esther. Melissa, of course, pushed Sunny aside so she was right smack in front of Beake Man.

"O–kay." Sunny's voice quavered.

"Just cut it in half. Sure. No problem," Vee said, not moving to do so.

"If you're not going to do it, you're just in the way." Melissa grabbed one of the knives and looked at Beake Man. "Might I have an apron and gloves? I wouldn't want mice guts on the pashmina jacket that I got in Paris, and I just had a mani today."

Esther heard a soft thud on the hard floor behind her.

Sunny turned. "Aneta? Aneta!"

The next sound was a grunt from Melissa and then the snick of a knife cutting through to the steel counter. *Urp.* The second flip of Esther's stomach dove deep and landed, squirming, then began to bounce upward. Turning, she tripped over Aneta on the floor. Staggering until she regained her balance, she sprinted to the carriage house door, hand over her mouth, shoulders jerking.

Melissa's words grated behind her. "Esther's just not cut out for this work, is she?"

Esther made it to the outside and right of the carriage house.

"Oh dear, I was afraid of this." The Bird Lady's voice penetrated Esther's emptying of her stomach. She patted Esther on the back, helping her ease back to a cross-legged position on the damp grass when it was over. "When people want to help wild birds, they often forget what wild birds eat."

Esther focused on breathing in and out through her nose. When she became aware of the mud on her shoes, she made a note she'd have to be sure to take them off in the garage. Her mother would scream for sure if she tracked that much mud in the house.

Aneta. Aneta on the ground. She tried to stand up, but her legs wouldn't hold her. Collapsing, she stammered, "A–A–neta fainted. On the floor. I'm such a bad friend. I jumped over her to get out and puke."

"Yes." The Bird Lady hunkered down so she was eye level with Esther. "I was just entering the carriage house when I saw her faint and you take off running. You ran past me. She's fine. Feeling a little light-headed, but fine. It doesn't make you a bad friend. Would you like to go back in now?"

No. Esther shuddered. Now, not only were frozen mice in there, but top halves and bottom halves of frozen dead mice. Had Sunny and Vee been able to pass the test? What did they think of her running out and abandoning them?

"I—I. . ." If she went back in, Melissa would make fun of her as sure as Esther's peanut butter and honey sandwich was spewed out on the grass. If she didn't go back in, though, Melissa might somehow, some way, take her place. Melissa's clipped words came back to her. *"Not up to the work."* This final project of the S.A.V.E. Squad. At least the S.A.V.E. Squad with Esther in it.

"I have to go back in. I have to see what's going on." She wiped her mouth once more with the small towel the Bird Lady had produced from her many-pocketed barn coat. "Melissa. . ."

"I get the notion that Melissa is not a friend to you four, then?"

Esther nodded. She remembered where her arms and legs were. In another moment, she had wriggled to her feet, and it seemed she would stay upright. Her stomach felt like she'd been punched. Maybe she'd never eat again.

The Bird Lady was eyeing her sort of like the buzzard in the nearby flight cage, with her head cocked to the side and tipped, looking at Esther with one eye. "There's more here you're not telling, isn't there?"

Esther nodded again. Should she tell her secret to the Bird Lady? Blurt out that she had to move when school was out? Had to make sure the S.A.V.E. Squad had one last project to save *something* so they wouldn't forget her? Would Melissa take her place now since Esther couldn't chop up a mouse?

She felt miserable.

The Bird Lady sat back with a thump on the ground, crossing her legs and wrapping her long arms around her knees. For an old lady, she seemed pretty flexible.

"I—I have—to move." The first words jerked out. "I wanted to be in the S.A.V.E. Squad forever. I'm afraid the girls will forget me when I leave. They won't like me anymore." The moment the last word was out, she panicked. Backing away from Beverly Beake, she whispered, "You can't tell anyone. It will ruin everything."

"My dear girl, when are you planning to tell them?" Beverly's long face grew longer with her opened mouth.

When? Never? Today? It was all so confusing. "I don't know, but I will," she replied, staring at the ground.

"Come. Let's walk back in and see what's going on." The Bird Lady extended her hand to Esther then tucked her and Esther's hands into one of the bellows pockets. With the chilly air outside, the pocket felt like a hug.

Following a few moments of friendly silence, Beverly moved the subject away from Esther, for which Esther was grateful. "I know Byron is really bothered by the birds being shot," Bird Lady said as they walked. "No evidence they were shot with a gun."

Esther didn't hear anyone shrieking or yelling. Had Sunny and Vee passed the test? Or had they also fainted, and Melissa had stepped over them to do the work and show Beake Man that she was the best?

"Then hit with what? Who does he think did it?" Esther swallowed a lump in her throat as they stepped nearer and nearer to the big sliding door. She wished she hadn't left Aneta. About as much as she also wished she hadn't thrown up. Her mouth tasted yucky.

"Oh, he has no idea, poor darling." Her face looked worried. "I don't like him to worry. I'm afraid it will affect his recovery."

This was a perfect time to find out more about what happened to Beake Man. As Esther opened her mouth to ask, the doors rolled apart and Sunny, Vee, and Melissa spilled out, talking excitedly. Aneta dragged behind, looking pale.

"I would never have thought either of you had the guts to do it," Melissa was saying, bumping shoulders between Vee and Sunny like they were now BFFs.

Uh-oh. The knot of ick tightening inside Esther this time had nothing to do with cutting up mice and everything to do with losing her spot on the S.A.V.E. Squad.

"Hey, Esther!" Sunny darted ahead and threw her arms around Esther. "Are you okay? Aneta's okay. Vee and I did it!" She twirled around and around.

"Not that it was so great." Vee was not smiling, and her glance over at Melissa made Esther feel better. So. Vee didn't trust Melissa saying nice things. Good. They would have to tell Sunny to watch out. Sunny probably thought Melissa had changed while she was living in Paris. *No way*, Esther thought.

Byron Beake was the last to exit the carriage house. The doors rolled smoothly and only made the littlest thud when they connected. He turned to slide the iron bolt into the ground hole. She was beginning to like the Beake Man, even with his test. He didn't want the doors to slam because it would frighten the owls and the other birds.

"You girls did all right," he said gruffly as he passed them all. His gaze flickered over Esther. "You okay then?"

Heat exploded up from the base of Esther's neck. She nodded, too curious to stare at his face to drop her gaze in embarrassment. What would it be like to be so different from everyone?

The afternoon light was fading with the trees around the carriage house taking on a mysterious-house-in-a creepy-forest look. Once the group passed, she turned to fall in step with Aneta and the Bird Lady.

Aneta had yet to utter a word. Esther reached over and squeezed her hand.

"You okay?" she asked.

Aneta nodded and turned toward her, big tears perched on the rim of her blue eyes. "I was not brave. A Jasper is brave."

"I puked," Esther said. "As in majorly emptied my guts. How brave is that?"

Aneta's shoulders twitched, followed by a tiny gulpy chuckle.

Then a bigger snort, then she was laughing.

With Esther's own chuckles, the sick knot untied. The Bird Lady was laughing. She stepped between the girls and clasped their hands. Her hand was warm and dry and had hard spots on them like she worked hard with her birds. While laughing, the idea popped into Esther's head. *She* would find that—that Awful Person. She—and Aneta—would find the one who tried to hurt the yellow-eyed birds. That would be as important or, as a sneaky voice inserted, *more* important than cutting up mice.

"I will tell you a secret those other girls do not know," Beverly Beake said in a lowered voice.

The girls leaned in to hear.

"I can't feed the raptors either."

Aneta's mouth, opened in an *O*, matched Esther's.

The Bird Lady chuckled a chirpy giggle. "I really wanted to help with the raptors when I was younger over in England. I begged and begged my brother—him already licensed, you see—and was getting rather peeved with him that he wouldn't let me. Finally, after months of pushing me off, he said he would give me a test." She arched her eyebrows at the two girls, then nodded at the dawning understanding that rolled across Esther's face.

"Like he tested us!" So it wasn't because he was just being mean and wanted them to fail.

"It was not to be mean?" Aneta was on the same page. Her face brightened. "Did you faint?"

Pressing her lips together as though she were trying to swallow back a laugh, the Bird Lady bobbed her head up and down. "And I threw up." Her laugh burst out. The three hee-heed so loudly, the first group, nearly to the back french windows that led into the breakfasting room, turned to stare. Windows next to the many-paned french doors stood floor to ceiling with their crank-out glass. Today, of course, they weren't open. Esther shivered in her coat, warming and chilling as the excitement built over what she would tell the S.A.V.E. Squad. She would find That Person.

"What's so funny?" Sunny wanted to know, bouncing back to them.

"It is okay that I fainted," Aneta explained, like it was supposed to be clear.

Esther smiled. "I have an idea on what we"—she gestured toward Aneta—"can do while you guys help with the owls." She looked straight at Melissa. "I'll tell you when it's just the Squad."

Did Melissa's eyes narrow ever so slightly like Vee's did when she was headed into a Vee Stare? It didn't matter. No way was she going to tell the girls when Melissa was around that the Squad should find That Awful Person and make sure no other owls got hit with whatever.

"Oh, I'm glad you found *something* you can do, Esther," Melissa replied.

Suddenly the Squad was on alert.

Sunny stopped bouncing around Aneta, Esther, and the Bird Lady and stood with her head cocked, looking back and forth between Esther and Melissa. Vee's dark eyebrows were almost touching, she was frowning so hard. Aneta whispered, "Oh dear."

With a dismissive shrug of her shoulder, Melissa glided up the two steps that led to the french doors. "Oh, girls, my dad is sending his driver to take me home. Why don't I give you all a ride home? We"—her glance slid quickly toward Esther and then away—"*might* all fit."

Her stomach flip-flopped. Esther knew exactly what Melissa meant. There would be room for the other girls, but not for her. She blurted, "Oh, that's okay, Melissa. My mom is coming to take us home anyway. See you later."

Hopefully a lot later.

Melissa's ride arrived moments later after she spoke rudely into her smartphone. Before stepping into what Esther's brothers had previously identified as a Cadillac Escalade, she cast her glance around to Sunny and Vee. "You girls sure?"

They shook their heads and stepped closer to Aneta and Esther. Then the big black vehicle splashed its way down the muddy driveway.

Esther's satisfaction at seeing Melissa depart without a single member of the S.A.V.E. Squad in that fancy car morphed into full-blown panic. Three very bad things trashed her triumph. The first one was humongous—*she hadn't yet asked her mother if she would pick them up.* Two—her mom would drive their minivan, which was older than any of the Squad's cars and way older than the big black SUV that had just left.

The four girls were quiet, watching the back end of the vehicle. Then Vee said, still looking down the road, "Your mom doesn't know she's picking us up, does she?"

"N–nope." Esther's lower lip wobbled.

Aneta gasped, a hand flying to her mouth. "Gram does not like it when I ask her to do something when you all are around."

"Yeah," Sunny chimed in. "My mom's reaction to that is usually no and a long talk about putting her on the spot." She took her gaze from the long driveway, patted Esther's shoulder, and said cheerfully, "You're toast."

That wasn't the worst thing. The third worst thing? Sidney would be in that minivan with her irate mom. No way would her mother leave Siddy home with Toby.

Throwing up now seemed like the best part of this day.

Chapter 12

Hanging Around

W"here do we start?" Aneta and Esther stood in front of the tree on Friday, where they had discovered the two injured owls the previous Saturday. And nearly got struck by lightning. Their bikes lay on the ground behind the tree. Esther had the monocular Byron had said she could use. She'd about dropped it in surprise the day he handed it to her with the gruff admonition to "not bash it around, if you please." It was like binoculars only it had one lens instead of two. It made Esther feel like a pirate. She held it to her eye and looked up into the tree. No more owls. No pirates either.

Sunny and Vee had ridden in to the estate to help prepare the bird food for the day. No sign of Melissa. Esther hoped she'd already lost interest.

Today they hadn't even needed their raincoats and wore low hikers, jeans, and school hoodies. Esther had borrowed Toby's black beanie because it seemed a good clue-finding hat. Aneta wore winter gloves she called her clue-finding gloves. She was also wearing a bright yellow Cunningham Academy sweatshirt. So much for sneaking up on anyone.

As Esther left the house, Mom had been reading Siddy a *Hey, Imogene!* book. Sidney's high-pitched voice was shouting "There is always a clue!" Imogene hollered this at one point or another in every *Hey, Imogene!* story. Sometimes the just-past-three-year-old would walk around saying it for days, looking for clues in places there couldn't possibly be any. Like the bottom of the dirty clothes hamper. *Well, why not do an Imogene?*

Hands on her hips, she said matter-of-factly, "First, we look all around the tree. There must be something there besides feathers, gravel, and dirt."

The two girls circled the tree hunkered down in spy mode. Esther spotted rolled dirt. At least that's what it looked like. Some soft fluff caught in it waved in the breeze. Whipping out her plastic zip-top bags from the kitchen, she used a twig to roll three of them into the bag. Then she stuck the bag in her pocket.

"What is that?" Aneta inquired, straightening up.

"I think, not positive, that these are owl pellets."

"Pellets."

"What owls don't use up comes out the other end."

"Oh. Why do we want them?"

Esther laughed. "I don't know—just wanted to use my zip-top evidence bags like a detective." Maybe Byron could use them. Okay, now what? She stared at the ground, puffing her cheeks in and out. Sunny and Vee were doing important work. She and Aneta needed something *big*. When Esther groaned and rose, Aneta was regarding the upper branches of the tree. The immense tree. Esther's heart sank. Having a clutching feeling over Aneta's next words, Esther prayed what her father called a "grenade prayer." Small and, she hoped, powerful. *Please, oh please, Lord.* She squeezed her eyes shut.

"I think we will have to climb the tree to see what there is to see."

Esther opened her eyes and lowered her shoulders from her ears. Esther had climbed trees a time or two. Her discovery? *She did not like to climb trees.* She was short. Her legs were short, her arms were short, and her stomach got in the way. She liked to read under trees, and if she had her own iPad like she was always suggesting to her parents, she would have liked surfing the Net under the tree. But *climbing* trees? No.

"There must be something else we can do." Esther walked around the tree again hoping to find something magically deposited from the last circle.

"Except I do not know how to climb a tree." Aneta looked embarrassed. "Show me, and I will learn."

Esther sighed. "Okay, you see that branch that's just above your head? Wrap your arms around that and walk your feet up the tree until you can squoogle around the branch to sit on the branch like a horse."

In another moment Aneta was in the tree, beaming triumph. "Now I can climb a tree! Wait until I tell Mom and Gram and The Fam." Aneta motioned her to join her in the branches.

"Now you come up, Esther. I can see forever."

"I can't." Esther's words sounded angry and ready for a fight. "My arms are too short to reach the branches. My legs are too short to swing up into the tree. I'm too fat."

Bracing herself on branches, Aneta swung out into the air and dropped lightly to the ground next to her friend. "Then I'll help you." She looked at the two mountain bikes behind the tree. "I will put one of these bikes against a tree and really hold it hard, and you climb up that way."

Sure. She could break her arms and legs, too. This last mission of the S.A.V.E. Squad was going to be the death of her. At least after she moved, the Squad wouldn't have to worry about somebody being too fat to do their adventures with them.

"There." Aneta had placed her bike, the taller of the two, against the tree. "I will help you onto the seat, and you can stand up from there."

How had that tree sprouted twice as tall since Aneta first climbed it? Esther knew she couldn't back down. Since she couldn't cut up a mouse and Melissa could, and if she couldn't climb the tree, that didn't make her much use for anything. So climb the tree she would. The thought "or die trying" came to her mind, but she pushed it down into the pool of nerves jiggle-jouncing around in the bottomest bottom of her stomach.

As she lifted her leg up toward the seat, she once again discovered she was too short. She couldn't get on the stupid seat to climb into the tree. She was about to turn around and tell Aneta to just forget it, she wasn't good for anything and she might as well quit the Squad before she moved, when she saw Aneta had dropped to all fours like a pony.

"What are you doing?" Esther swallowed past the lump in her throat.

"Stand on my back, and then you can stand on the seat."

"I'm too heavy. I'll smush you if I stand on your back."

"Not if you move really fast. One step on my back. One step onto this seat. One jump. Pull yourself into the tree."

Easy for her long-legged friend to say. Esther did as she was told, and in a moment, with less skin on her elbows and knees and calves, she was breathing hard and in the tree. Not happy. But in the tree.

Since Aneta had been so nice about the tree-climbing help, Esther didn't correct her that you couldn't see forever. But you could see a really long ways. The black-iron fence ran out of sight to the left. In front of her now, the woods of the Beake estate spread out. In the distance, she could see the thin outlines of the flight cages, could see the edge of the carriage house.

"Sunny and Vee must still be helping Mr. Beake." Aneta stood on a branch that grew out straight from the trunk. It put her waist at Esther's head. Esther was standing on the branch with scratches and scraped-off bark. Maybe it was the branch the owls had been sitting on when they'd been hit?

Remembering the blood and the pathetic sounds the little owls had made that Saturday reignited Esther's determination. No more messing around. She and Aneta would find that—that Awful Person. Mr. Beake would be happy, the Squad would help the owls fly again, and the last mission—here her throat prickled—would be a fantastic victory.

Next to "there's always a clue," another of Imogene's favorite sayings was, "If you get down, look up!" Well, they were up and looking. Pulling out the monocular, she peered right. The long driveway to the mansion and forest to the right of that. As she peered toward the left, she noted a cluster of buildings—almost a straight line out from where the birds fell.

She pointed. "Look, Aneta. There's a farm over there. Funny, I've never seen it from the road when we ride to Uncle Dave's ranch. It must be right before that last curve to the ranch." Rolling the top dial, she zoomed in and out but could see nothing more clearly.

"Maybe they have a clue!" Placing her hands carefully, Aneta stepped onto a branch that took her closer to the spikes of the fence. "Maybe someone saw something." Another couple of sidesteps took her to the branch that protruded straight from the main trunk of the tree and hung out over onto Beake property about six feet off the ground. The metal spikes were now behind and underneath her.

73

Those spikes made Esther think of the Middle Ages and weapons of warfare. No way did she want to fall on those spikes.

"Be careful, Aneta!" Esther narrowed her eyes. "Maybe that's where that Awful Person lives." The fastest way to get there was. . . Glancing down, she gulped. She didn't want to think about the fastest way to get there.

"Here I go!" As gracefully as a ballerina, Aneta dropped onto the piney ground. "Come on, Esther!"

Esther edged her right foot out on to the same branch. Leaned her weight onto it. Tucked the monocular in her side pocket. The branch swayed slightly. She removed her foot. *I can't do it.*

"Hurry, Esther. We must do our part. Once we have our clue, we can tell Sunny and Vee. Then the Squad will be together on this!"

"Let me just think for a minute—don't rush me." Esther reviewed the situation. She could slide back down the tree and lose more skin on her legs and elbows. Then she could ride on her bike with bleeding arms and legs down the road to where the turnoff had to be for this bunch of buildings.

Or they could wait until Sunny and Vee came back out on their bicycles, Aneta could walk out the gate, and they could all ride down the road to the turnoff. She could already imagine Vee's upraised eyebrows at that turtle-slow plan. She moved several more steps out on the branch until she was the same distance Aneta had been when she jumped. Sunny would flat out ask why she didn't just—

Jump.

While Aneta continued to wait, Esther's eyes flickered back and forth as though seeing each choice. If she jumped, she could sprain her ankle and then they wouldn't be able to investigate the buildings. If she jumped, she could die and then that would be the end of the last S.A.V.E. Squad mission. If she—

"Esther!" Aneta was finally sounding impatient. Aneta who was *never* impatient.

Esther jumped. The ground came up to meet her. It hadn't been that far. All she had to do was land like Aneta told her—like a frog and then roll into a somersault if she hit the ground really hard.

Like a frog.

Somersault.

But what was this? Her body was falling *backward* a little. This was not good. She windmilled her arms. Backward was where greedy spikes of the fence waited. In another second, the neck of her hoodie shot to her chin, gagging her. Her hood! It was snagged on what could only be one or more of the spikes. Her backside bumped the fence, and there she hung, clawing frantically at the neck of her sweatshirt.

"Ahhh." It was a croak. With both her hands pulling down, her breathing returned to normal. Sort of.

The question now? How to get off the spikes.

"Esther!" Aneta stood about a foot below, jumping up and down, waving her hands. "Are you okay, Esther?"

Esther's shoulders jammed up under her ears made looking down impossible. No, she was not okay. About the only good thing about this entire thing was that Melissa was not around to see it.

"Hey! Esther!" called a familiar, smirky voice.

This was so not *living the yayness*.

"What *are* you doing?" More than one familiar voice. Sunny and Vee.

As Sunny would say, this was a major ughness. For a crazy second, Esther was almost glad she was leaving town.

Sunny and Vee sprinted on their bikes from the road to the tree. Melissa was hanging out of the Cadillac moving through the gate, her voice quite clear. "Really, Esther, is that the best you can do?"

Chapter 13

Not Even a Little Funny

*Y*ou don't think it was even a little funny?" Sunny was spinning in front of the other three, directing her question at a grumpy Esther.

"I wouldn't think so if I had to leave *my* hoodie on the spike." Vee had come up with the idea that Esther put up both her arms and slide out of the hoodie. That had released her, but not her hoodie. None of the girls were tall enough to tweak it down. No branches long enough nearby either. Now the wind had picked up. Esther wrapped her arms around herself. *Lord, why does this only happen to me?*

With the now-familiar bitterness pinching again, Esther's glare was her answer to Sunny. While Esther had been glad to see the other two girls as she wriggled on the fence spikes, it seemed that tight spot deep inside flamed angry every time one of the Squad members opened their mouth. She'd even yelled at Aneta when Aneta tried to push her up high enough on the spike to make the hood let go. *What is wrong with me?*

"I would not have liked to have Melissa say that to *me*." Aneta slung an arm around Esther's T-shirted shoulders.

It never would have happened to you. Or Vee. Or Sunny. Just me.

The knot twisted tighter. She walked faster. They needed a clue, they needed it now, and she wanted to be the one to find it. So there.

"I think Melissa isn't so bad, after you get to know her." Sunny skipped farther ahead and spun. "I mean, she'll, like, never be my best friend, but she likes to help the owls and the other birds. Could a person be mean and do that?"

Esther waited for Vee's reply. Vee and she often butted heads, yet Esther liked how Vee told it the way it was.

"I don't trust her," was all Vee said, but it was enough that Esther's shoulders lowered a bit from around her ears. Her sore shoulders that had been *jacked up by the hoodie*. By the hoodie *still on the fence*, blowing in the increasing wind. The wind that was *very cold*, thank you very much. She shivered.

With Esther trotting to keep up with the other girls, they were covering the distance to the building quickly.

"How are the owls doing?" Aneta wanted to know, smoothing down the long blond strands the wind picked up and tossed around.

"Has Melissa gotten to touch them?" Esther added. "Probably. She gets to do everything." She pulled out the plastic bag. "We found owl pellets."

Another look between Sunny and Vee. The other two agreed that Byron would be glad to get them, as it would tell him more about the wounded owls.

"Except it doesn't tell us anything about that Awful Person," Vee commented.

Pinch.

"Nobody gets to touch them. Beake Man hopes to release both of them." Sunny walked backward to face them while she was talking. Esther knew if she'd done that, she'd trip and break her head. "Did you know that wild bird helpers aren't supposed to name the birds?"

Yes, *of course* Esther knew that. When she'd checked out how to help wild raptors, she'd learned that "imprinting" was dangerous to a wild bird. Once an animal or bird connected to a human, it made them dangerous to themselves in the wild and to humans. She just hadn't had a chance to tell them with the Squad busted into two groups, and she and Aneta doing the hard part. She most *certainly* hadn't told them she had gone ahead and named one of the owls anyway.

She'd only named Bubo, the smaller owl, because she knew with all the blood that day they'd found them, he would end up staying. Like she wanted to stay. He would get to be in on all the fun of the bird education shows that the Bird Lady did, like the Squad would have the fun of more animal rescues. She was different from Bubo in that they'd do those things without her.

So not fair.

Pinch.

"Yeah," Vee took up the lecture, with a hint of a smile in her voice. "He told us that the day Aneta fainted and—well, Esther had to leave."

Sure. Make her sound like the one Squader that couldn't take it. The tightness in her tummy squeezed.

"I bet he said that 'cause he thinks we're silly girls who want to wrap them up in baby blankets and have a tea party with them," Vee finished, curling her lip.

In a few more steps they would break through the end of the trees that fringed the open space where the buildings were. That's when Esther first heard the sounds.

"What's that?" she asked.

"Sounds like a bunch of people talking," Vee said.

"No, it's not that. Not people," Sunny disagreed.

"Chickens. It's chickens," Esther said, listening hard and pulling the monocular from her side cargo pocket.

Peeking through the pines, the girls saw pens of chickens way off. The different feathered birds scratched here and there, pecking at whatever was on the ground.

"Esther was right," Sunny breathed.

Why was it such a surprise she was right? Esther rolled her eyes. Now what would Imogene do with a chicken farm? How was a chicken farm going to help with finding clues about that Awful Person? Smothering a sigh, she remembered none of the other Squad adventures had been this hard to figure out.

While Sunny spilled what she remembered her uncle Dave had said about some guy opening a free-range chicken farm a few months ago and that he didn't seem to know much about chickens or free range, Aneta and Vee squatted down to listen. Each traced sticks through the pine needles. Esther remained a few steps apart, staring at the farm through the monocular. *She* was staying focused.

What did she care about a chicken farmer and if he knew about raising chickens? The girls kept forgetting the plan was to *help the owls be safe*. The tightness in her tummy gave her a nasty taste in her mouth. Maybe they didn't care if they solved the mystery.

She was about to turn to them and yell, "Why don't you care?" when she caught a flash of something larger than a chicken. Before her brain could tell her legs to crouch, her legs collapsed on their own, thumping her on the pine needles. A man. A man staring right at her while she'd been staring right at him!

"Uh, guys," she said, her breath coming in fast bursts, interrupting Sunny who had detoured into a long story about Uncle Dave getting ready to take Aneta's mother out.

"—slicked back his hair, and you know his hair. It looked so—what, Esther?" Sunny sighed and paused.

"We've been spotted. He's coming for us." She wasn't sure she wanted to tell them what the man was carrying.

Chapter 14

Save the Beake Man!

Run!"

"Run fast!"

Were they kidding? They would all make it back to the mansion, and she'd be stumbling right in the guy's way. Esther needed a different plan, a better plan. She ran along behind them, looking for a bush, a cave, a secret passageway. Nothing. She sighed and started looking for something else.

A tree to climb.

The man passed them and was nearly out of sight in the trees before the girls blew out the breaths they'd been holding. Sunny, Aneta, and Vee sat high in an evergreen tree, Esther on the lowest branch of another.

"Esther, you didn't tell us he was carrying a *hunting rifle*." Vee sagged against a big branch behind her.

"For pizza sakes, we get into trouble!" Shaking her head, Sunny stood up, balancing on a thick branch highest up. She'd been the quickest to scramble up the tree when Esther changed their plan. Aneta was across from her.

"I am glad I had climbed a tree already today," she said. "It was a very good opportunity."

The other two laughed at Aneta's use of *opportunity*, her adoptive mother's favorite word. Esther, who had her arms wrapped around the branch she was straddling like a pony, said not a word. If she opened her mouth, she might fall out of the tree and bounce a couple of times on the ground. This had to be the worst Squad adventure ever. Sure, they had had trouble before, but never had she messed up so many times.

They could do better without you. The thought wriggled up her stomach again. *I am the worst on the Squad. I can't run fast, I'm no good at climbing trees, and I can't chop up a mouse.* But she was so smart in school. She could find things on the Internet. Once those snaky thoughts slithered into her heart though, more followed and repeated, *They're better off without you.*

"Um, guys," Sunny said, looking down at them from her perch. "While we were in the carriage house, Vee and I heard Byron on the phone with some guy who was really angry."

Poor Byron. He'd been nice enough to let her use the monocular. Esther grabbed for her pocket. *Whew. Still there.* So were the owl pellets. Was that man going after Byron?

"We've got to save Byron!" she yelped, jerked, and fell right out of the tree.

Thump!

Ow. More skin off her elbows.

The worst Squader.

As soon as the rest of the girls descended the tree—losing no

82

skin—they trotted after the man. Vee checked her pocket to make sure she still had her tiny notebook and pen.

"We need a plan," she said.

"You can't write in your notebook while we're hurrying," Esther snapped, stumbling again on the uneven ground. She hated, hated, *hated* hurrying, even though she knew they were saving Beake Man.

"I know that." Vee shot her the Vee Stare. "What's up with you?"

"In case nobody noticed, I am all scraped up, I'm limping, and— *oowf!*" Something leaning against a large stone sent her sprawling on the softish, fragrant, piney ground. Could she just please stop sprawling on the ground? *Pinch.*

The three turned and hurried back to help her up.

"Look, Esther—look what you tripped over!" Aneta held up a metal something with a dangling—what?

"Slingshot." Sunny put her hands on her knees, drawing in a couple of slow breaths. "For pizza sakes, Aneta and Vee, you guys have such long legs!" She collapsed on the ground, only to spring up again. "I bet—"

"That Awful Person used that to hit the owls!" Esther interrupted. Sunny bobbed her head in agreement.

"And that guy came this way and must have dropped it!" Vee thrust her hands in her jeans pockets and kicked around the area where Esther had splatted. "I don't see anything else."

With her knee smarting enough to make her eyes sting, Esther shifted from one leg to another. "Then we better get going." Stuffing the slingshot in her other bellows pocket, she finished, "If that guy would zing baby—"

" —'teenage,' Beake Man said." Vee turned to run again and missed Esther's glare. "But yeah, if he's mad enough at Beake Man, he could zap him with something bigger!"

Esther remembered how gentle Beake Man was with the birds, how he made sure he didn't slam the carriage house doors. *Okay. Stop complaining!* she told herself sternly. They had to save Beake Man. Grunting, she slapped at the slingshot in her pocket and said, "C'mon."

They heard the two men before they saw them between the carriage house and the mansion.

"I'm sick of you teaching your killer birds to practice on my chickens!" that Awful Person roared, reaching up to poke a finger at Beake Man's skinny chest. He was quite a bit shorter than Byron.

"If you'd take your blinkers off, you'd see it's not my birds playing havoc with your chickens!" Beake Man's voice, though thinner and a little gaspy, sounded equally angry.

The girls hid behind two big trees that shared a massive trunk. Sunny on her knees with Aneta crouched over her. Vee peeking from the other side with Esther sitting cross-legged and peering out through the pine branches that grew close to the ground. She pulled out an uncomfortable pinecone from beneath and seconds later had an idea.

"Hey," she hissed, holding up the pinecone. "We've got to break this up before they start fighting." If the Bad Guy hit him in the face or bumped Byron's mask, bad things might happen to Byron's face. The Squad was becoming very fond of Byron's face.

Esther tipped to all fours and pushed herself to her feet. They had to move quickly. Spy Mode.

"Nothing like this happened before you moved in!" that Awful Person was saying.

The girls looked at the two men. Esther shared her plan, gesturing with the pinecone.

"Spy Mode then!" Esther directed the girls to slink from tree to tree until they were on the side and behind that Awful Person.

"Take off your sweatshirts." Sunny demonstrated why with her hoodie that had a picture of a horse on it.

Good idea.

Now that Awful Person was telling Beake Man he ought to punch him in the face. Beake Man was backing up, fists clenched.

I bet he wants to pop that ole Awful Person. Esther knew just how he felt. Someone had made fun of Siddy once when her little brother was doing something strange. Good thing Mom had been there and said something about rising above the situation. Esther hadn't liked it, but it helped her not hit the kid, which was a good thing. The kid had been a lot bigger than her.

"Brilliant!" Vee said, stripping off her Moby Perkins Elementary red-and-yellow hoodie.

"The Squad thinks of everything," Aneta approved and followed suit with her bright Cunningham Academy hoodie.

For a very quick second, Esther wished her hoodie wasn't still swinging off the spikes out front. But—she grinned—*she* had the slingshot. "Once you're in position, I'll give the signal." The girls nodded and dropped to scuttle like monkeys, using their arms to keep their balance so low to the ground. In a blink, they were in position.

She looked right. Vee was filling her makeshift ammo holder with pinecones. Looking left, she noted Aneta and Sunny doing the same.

"You can use my pinecones," Vee whispered.

Esther nodded. "Right. Time to act." She raised both arms up, pressing them against her ears. Peering around her arms, she smiled. Vee was ready. She turned left. Sunny and Aneta nodded. They would attack that Awful Person's left side.

She brought her arms down hard, squatting quickly to load the slingshot.

Chapter 15

Imogene Moves

Esther loaded and pitched the first pinecone, a solid, unopened one. Playing endless catch with her brothers—and especially Siddy who was remarkable for his age with catching, though not throwing—she had an arm. She released the rubber sling, and the pinecone whizzed through the afternoon sun breaking through the drizzle and smacked that Awful Person on the neck. *Ha!* Surely an Imogene move.

He turned in her direction.

Sunny's voice hollered from the left. A second pinecone, larger and heavier looking than Esther's, thunked that Awful Person's shoulder. Whipping his head around, he started for Sunny and Aneta. They shrieked and ducked back into the protection of the trees.

"You there! Back off those girls!"

That Awful Person stopped and turned to face the taller man, sneering. "What is this, your security force?" But he didn't continue after the girls.

Esther stepped from her spot, slingshot in hand. Vee joined her, muttering, "I didn't even get to pitch mine. I wanted to nick his ear."

They joined Beake Man, facing that Awful Person who glared at them, clenching his fists. His eyebrows shot upward. Darting forward, he snatched the slingshot from Esther's hand. "Where did you get this? This isn't yours!"

Esther opened her mouth to tell him just where she got it and how it now proved that he was the zapper of the poor owls when Byron raised his hand and spoke. His voice, though quiet, sliced through the tension in the backyard.

"Enough. Take your leave. You are not welcome here."

That Awful Person muttered. Esther thought she heard him say "she" and figured he was griping about her breaking up his plan to punch Beake Man in the face. The Squad had done it again. That slingshot had helped this time instead of hurting.

Circling Byron, the girls peppered him with questions. "Are you all right?" "Is your face okay?" "We had lots more pinecones!" "I wish I'd had a chance to shoot mine!"

Aneta looked worried. Esther knew she was wondering "now what?" after shooting someone, even with a pinecone. Esther hoped Aneta would see all this as an "opportunity."

For a moment, Beake Man closed his eyes and tipped his head back. It was a familiar gesture, and Esther's frown slipped into a smile. Frank had that expression whenever he was around the girls for very long. "You like us now, don't you." She stepped forward and patted his arm.

Aneta's big smile broke out.

Sunny spun. "I knew you would. Nobody hates us for very long."

Only Vee looked reluctant. "Except Melissa. She just keeps hating us."

Sunny opened her mouth then closed it, shaking her head. Esther wondered why. Was she going to say that Melissa wasn't so bad? That maybe she'd changed? Maybe Sunny wished Melissa could become a

Squad member? No, she wouldn't. She *couldn't*.

"I think you're bonkers, but your hearts are gold." Byron finally smiled. It was the first real smile they'd seen. It stretched slowly at first, like it wasn't used to being out and about, but then crawled wide and big. His teeth were large and white. He looked quite nice behind that mask. With a start, Esther realized she'd stopped being shocked when she looked at him.

"We couldn't let that Awful Per—guy hurt you." Aneta flushed, lowering her eyes and scanning the girls anxiously. She'd nearly let the name slip. Even though nobody had said "don't," the Squad seemed to sense that now was not the time to tell Byron that they had discovered the identity of the one who hurt the owls.

Vee checked the time on her ATP. "We've got to get going. It's almost five."

"Before you go"—Byron's voice faltered, like he wondered if he should say what he was going to say—"mightn't you like to peep at the owls on the camera?"

Vee looked at Aneta, whose eyes were wide with delight. Sunny looked at Esther. Esther clapped her hands.

Four voices shouted, "Mightn't we!"

Esther punched the code into the pad by the garage door, shucked her muddy sneakers, and pounded up the stairs. "Mom! Mom!"

Halfway up, she heard Siddy's delighted echo, "Mom! Mom!" and then "Esther is here. Hooray for Esther!" She stifled a groan. It was nice to be greeted when she got home, but her little brother didn't understand that shouting into her ear *hurt*.

At the top of the stairs, her mother, smiling, held Siddy back.

"What happened to make you so excited?"

"We saved Beake Man from that Awful Person!" Pausing with one hand on the wall and the other on the stair railing, Esther beamed up at her mom. "It was so cool. We used pinecones!"

Her mother waved her up. "C'mon up. I can't hold your brother off much longer. Tell us both." Holding her son with her left arm, she pointed to the living room with her right. "Fall into a chair and tell us."

After Esther braced herself, her mom let Siddy go, and her little blond-headed brother bounced the two steps and threw himself at her. There was never any doubt in Siddy's mind that someone would catch him. That worried Esther. What would happen when he went to school? Would he ever go to school, or was he too different?

She told the story in every exciting detail and then flopped against the worn plaid love seat. Siddy lost interest and headed toward his room down the hall.

"Esther! You didn't hurt him, did you?"

Esther shook her head.

"I would certainly like to meet the Beakes," her mom mused. "Your dad says they're great people, but different." She brightened. "I know. I'll invite them, you can invite the girls, and we'll have dinner here. Then"—she fixed a slanted fake-mad glare at her daughter—"you can tell the S.A.V.E. Squad about our moving."

Here? People here? In his room, Siddy alternated between chanting "Moving! Moving!" and "Esther's home! Hooray for Esther!" Sure. Let people think she lived in a crazy house.

"Oh, I don't know, Mom, the Beakes are kind of different. I don't know if they go to people's houses. The birds take a lot of time. Especially the owls. Byron let us see them through the camera and play with the robotic arm to feed them with the mother bird puppet.

It was so cool. I still wish I could be with Vee and Sunny and help feed them. I—"

"Esther."

"What?"

"You know what. . . You're avoiding my question."

"Oh." Where was Toby? Always underfoot, why would he pick today to hole up in his room?

"Moving! Moving! Esther is home! Hooray for Esther!"

Flinching a little at her brother's volume and high-piercing singsong, she said, "Because."

"Because why, Esther?" Her mother sounded a little puzzled, mixed with a lot of impatient.

Esther drew in a deep breath. Maybe her other brother would at last come and create some distraction. Glancing hopefully over at the hall, she didn't respond. If she said she didn't want the girls to be around Siddy, her mother would be hurt, and that would hurt Esther. So far, Siddy had pulled his rare silent act around them. Once he got comfortable with them. . . If she said yes to her mom's idea, her life as she knew it would be over. The girls would be happy she was leaving town with her crazy brother.

Silence filled the room while she struggled with no good options.

In a low voice, she said, "Because Siddy will yell something about us moving."

From down the hall, they heard, "Moving! Moving! Moving!"

Tipping her head toward her mother, Esther held out her hands as if to say, "See?"

Her mother uncrossed her legs and sat up straight.

Uh-oh.

"Moving! Moving! Moving!"

Esther shook her head.

"Esther Hannah Martin, when exactly are you going to tell your best friends in the whole world that you are moving at the end of this school year?"

Since her mother had used all of her names, Esther knew exactly what her mother thought about her not telling the Squad. If indeed they were her best friends, she thought, her mouth turning down. Maybe not, if Melissa had anything to say about it.

When would she tell them? If she waited much longer to answer her mother, she would get in trouble for not obeying.

Finally, a thought struck her, and she blurted, "The day we release the owls." The end of everything.

As soon as the words came out, the urgency rose so quickly to bring final evidence to Byron and the sheriff before the birds were released, she had to clamp her lips shut. Her mother would not understand. Finding the person who zapped Bubo and the other owl had been the first most important thing on the planet. Now that the Awful Person turned out to be the chicken farmer, the Squad needed more proof. Once they found it, then, forever after, to whatever terrible place Esther had to move, she would know she'd been the best Squader she could have been.

The girls would know it.

So would Melissa.

Siddy came thudding down the hall, and Esther allowed herself to be dragged to his room where she once again read another *Hey, Imogene!* book. In her head, while Imogene shouted "There's no messing with Imogene!" and finding the bad guys, Esther was plotting her own Imogene moves.

It was time for something her mother called *drastic*.

Chapter 16

Things Drag

"Drastic" took loads longer than Esther imagined.

On Saturday, the girls returned to the estate for Sunny and Vee's meal preparation. To entertain herself during that time, Esther unearthed Toby's slingshot to see if she could get Howard to run for special bird nuggets, after which the girls fully intended to coax Byron to leak further information about the chicken farmer that they could use to find evidence.

Instead, after Sunny, Vee, and Byron had cleaned and sanitized their hands, Byron seemed quite taken with the slingshot delivery.

"That might be brilliant to use for the owls. They would see the food move through air. Might help their instincts." He urged Esther to keep working with the buzzard so Byron could see the benefits.

Moments later, Esther was pouting. "I want Howard to run up and catch the nuggets, not wait until they're lying on the ground and then eat them. How's he going to get exercise that way?"

"Esther, Howard eats dead things. He's not much of a border collie." Byron's eyes glinted with humor. Their pinecone defense of him had thawed him considerably. He took them with him to a field way behind the right side of the mansion and released and recalled the peregrine falcon.

"They are beautiful." Aneta's head was tipped up, watching the falcon soar in the noonday sun. "The owls are so different, but also beautiful."

"Yes, and the owl talons have two thousand pounds of pressure per square inch to crush their prey after swooping down from the sky," Byron said.

"We get it, Byron. We can't make them pets," Vee said.

All eyes were on the clear sky to watch the incoming of the falcon. All eyes but Esther's. *People, we're on a* mission *here.* With her fists on her hips, she blurted, "Why does that chicken farmer not like you?"

Byron hesitated, then pulled his hand through his wispy hair. Esther didn't think he was going to answer. Then he said, "He started losing chickens, parts of chickens, finding pellets."

"But why blame you? There must be hawks and other raptors around." Vee eyed the falcon with a smile as it landed on Byron's outstretched, gloved arm.

"Timing, I must think," Byron said. "He said right after Beverly did her first show at the community center with birds of prey it started happening." He shrugged. "Before that, he didn't know I was here."

"I have another question, as long as we're asking questions," Sunny said as the group headed back to the estate where Beverly had promised scones for a snack. She had learned the girls weren't much on tea. "How did you hurt your face?"

"Took you a long time to ask that one!" he said with a grin.

"You've probably noticed this, but the S.A.V.E. Squad is very polite," Esther informed him.

He laughed hard at this, then sobered as he told the story in quick strokes. He had been an off-duty firefighter in another part of Oregon and encountered a fire at a wild-horse facility. Before help arrived, he had saved all but two of the horses, yet he had been burned badly in the face and hands. His throat had been burned inside, too.

So that's why he sounds like he's whispering! Esther listened closely as he continued. "My sister flew in from England to help me recover. She likes it here."

"Who started it? The fire, I mean?" Vee liked to know whose fault it was when stuff happened.

His light eyes moved from Squader to Squader. "Kids."

Esther spoke up. "That's why you hated us at first. 'Cause we're kids."

He spread out his hands in apology. "I thought you were all the same. These kids were part of some group who thought wild horses in corrals was a terrible thing. Silly barnies. The horses were starving, had been abandoned in a national forest. They were part of an adoption program."

By the end of that day, while the girls were pleased Byron no longer considered them trouble and they'd learned the story of his face, they had learned nothing that would help them with their case. Aneta said their only consolation was that the chicken farmer must know they were on to him and maybe wouldn't cause trouble.

"But how will we get more evidence unless he does something?" Esther complained, grumbling about the delay to the final project of the S.A.V.E. Squad. And her part in it.

School started up again, and for the rest of the week, just like Esther feared, the Squad saw little of each other, limited to video conferencing and e-mails due to differing school, church, family activities, and homework. *It's already beginning.* Esther moped at her house and actually told Siddy to "shut up" during one of his *Hey, Imogene!* yells and promptly lost her computer privileges until Saturday. Her stomach hurt a lot—that bitterness was twisting terribly. She wanted to cry but wouldn't let herself. It was all about this final project.

When the Squad finally regrouped at the estate the following Monday, Byron was engrossed in repairing a long rip in a screen in one of the flight cages.

"Silly bird must have gotten dancing around inside and let a talon go wild," he said, shaking his head.

Esther looked at the rip and then stepped forward to inspect the lock. Straightening, she turned an I-told-you-so face to the Squad. She suspected sabotage. Now maybe the rest of the Squad would see how they needed to ramp up their investigation and *do* something. Do what, Esther had no idea, but something *drastic*. The next step for that Awful Person might just be the carriage house where Bubo and his buddy were stashed.

Sunny, Vee, and Aneta crowded around the rip and took turns noting the scratches on the lock.

"Want to see how Beverly taught me to sew a screen?" he asked.

"Sew a screen like a dress?" Aneta wrinkled her brow.

"More like making a potholder, I should think," Byron replied. "Esther, be a love and run into the carriage house—quietly—and bring me a roll of wire in the basket near the door. Mind the birds."

Esther hurried away, cautiously rolled the heavy door aside, and flipped on the first bank of lights. The basket sat right where Byron said it would be—close enough to snatch, close the door, and run back to the others. She scooped up the roll of wire, and as she straightened, her gaze fell on the draped owl cage. Bubo and buddy.

What harm would it do to take a little peek at them? To see

them without having to look through a TV screen. She would be so very careful, holding back just a teensy bit of the canvas to see them in person—er, in *owl*. Surely they couldn't imprint on such a tiny glimpse.

Tiptoeing over to Bubo and his buddy's cage, Esther hesitated before lifting her hand toward the canvas. Her hand dangled inches from her goal. She would be the first of the Squad to see the owls up close, see their cute round yellow eyes that sometimes looked like they were cross-eyed.

Then her hand dropped to her side.

No.

Seeing them without the Squad was not right. Even if the whole Squad never got to look at them, she wasn't going to see them without the girls. Besides, she'd been told not to by Byron, and he knew best. How could she pray and ask the Lord to help her with stuff she didn't know if she wasn't going to play fair with what she *did* know? The tightness in her stomach relaxed more than it had in several days.

Now she really wanted to cry.

About everything.

Turning with the coil of wire in her hand, she walked softly toward the door, her head down. Moving was going to be so hard. She just wanted to solve this last case with the girls.

A quiet "ahem" broke into her sad thoughts. Flinging up her head, she saw Byron standing in the doorway, hands jammed in his work-pant pockets. What had he seen? Did he think she'd peeked at the owls?

"I—I. . ." She didn't get any further.

He made a little bow. "Well done, my girl. Nothing like being told not to—makes a chap *want to* ever so much."

"You saw—"

"The whole struggle." As they walked back to the girls who were mending the rip, Byron asked her, "What made you stop and not break my rule? You couldn't know I was there."

Esther shrugged. "I remembered Whose I was. I just forgot for a minute."

Chapter 17

The Gear for Drastic

Great news, Esther!" On the phone after school on Monday, Vee's voice rippled with excitement.

Esther's heart yanked itself up from the bottom where it had been flopping around since getting in trouble at home. Had Vee come up with an idea to get the final evidence to convince Byron? Esther hadn't yet done a single huge thing for the girls to remember her by. Only loser stuff like being a bad tree climber and throwing up instead of helping feed the owls. Like *that* was how she wanted them to remember her.

"Esther, you still there?"

"What's great?" Esther asked.

"Bill is letting us into his garage to open the boxes from his old jobs!"

That was it? Poking around in a garage? Esther stood up from the couch and with the phone to her ear walked to the sliding door and the back porch. Her two brothers were running around the yard pointing their light sabers at each other. Whatever Toby yelled, Siddy found sounds and phrases in them that he was pleased to repeat at the top of his lungs.

The Squad needed to be at Beake Man's poking around for clues. Boxes in a garage? Sounds like a trick to work. Her thoughts wound up like her class's gerbil when he got going on his wheel. It wasn't only a trick, it was *stupid*.

Half an hour later, Esther's opinion hadn't changed. The girls had converged on the detached garage that was larger than the house. Before Vee's mom had married Bill, he had built the house and the garage. You sure could tell he liked garages better. Maybe because it was easier to pile boxes higher.

If Sunny's uncle Dave's kitchen had seemed like tall stacks of boxes, they were shrimps compared to the tall *shelves* with stacks of boxes on them. Sunny danced around Bill in her excitement. Aneta's eyes danced, and Vee looked proud of her stepdad. All for a dumb garage with boxes, while clues lay waiting *somewhere* on the Beakes' property.

"You guys, don't you think we should head on over to the Beakes' place instead? I mean, it's stopped raining for a bit. We could look for clues." She edged toward the side door, looking over her shoulder, stopping before rounding the corner of another set of steel shelves.

Pausing in another circuit around Bill, Sunny shook her head. "That's the trouble with this project. There just aren't any clues!" She flung out her arms. "For pizza sake, I want to have fun today!"

"There might be a treasure in one of these boxes." Aneta headed for a metal box with straps around it. "You never know."

Vee poked Bill. "Okay, which box can we open first?" Waving to Esther, she continued, "C'mon, Esther! We'll go over later," then turned her back to better listen to Bill explain that he wanted them to have some fun since the owl project was going kind of rough.

You can say that again. Esther, lingering alone by the corner of the shelves, felt the hard pinch of bitterness. When she had chosen not to look at the owls, the knot had eased, but the feeling hadn't lasted. The Squad didn't care about the owls, about Esther leaving, about the Squad at all. A quiet voice inside mentioned that the girls didn't *know* she was leaving, didn't *know* why she was so desperate to solve the case. Esther ignored the voice. Her hurt was growing stronger, and it wasn't fair to try to stop it. She turned to go. She'd go alone. She'd find the clue, solve the mystery, and Beake Man would be so grateful he'd let her—and only her—launch the second owl back to freedom.

"Guys! Look!"

Esther whirled at the high-pitched excitement in Sunny's voice. The redhead, her curls bouncing every which way, was holding up a—*a what?*—high over her head like a trophy.

"What—what is it?" Aneta walked around Sunny, her head tipped to the side.

Bill folded his arms over his chest, grinned, then said to Vee, "Do you know what it is?"

Vee came in close, looked at what was in Sunny's hand, and bent over, rummaging through what remained in the steel box. "Goggles!" she said, straightening with her arms full of straps and vacant black eyepieces. "But what kind?" She turned to Bill. "Spill, Bill. *Just what kind of jobs did you do?*"

Bill laughed the infectious laugh that made the girls—with the exception of Esther—laugh in return. "Are you telling me a squad like the S.A.V.E. Squad doesn't know what these are? Nobody knows?"

A chuckle slowly buzzed its way up through the tension in Esther. She headed toward the group. *She* knew what they were because she'd done a report for school and had found it on the Internet. Not only did she know what they were, but she knew how to use them for the drastic thing the Squad needed to do to get the final evidence on that Awful Person.

"Hurry," Esther tossed the words over her shoulder, hitching her pace to a trot. She'd laid down her bike on the front lawn of the estate and was now beat feeting it to the front door. An impatient glance showed the rest of the Squad close behind, but not close enough. Now that they had the night-vision goggles from one of Bill's boxes, they had to somehow get permission to stay until after dark to practice. Then, other nights, to stand guard. Time was running out.

It was Monday. Surely the owls would be released soon, and then nobody but her would care. And she wasn't convinced that Melissa had lost interest in the Squad, even though she no longer helped with the birds. What if she already talked to the girls about taking Esther's place and the girls hadn't told her?

School would be over the second week of June, and then Esther's life would be over. No more Squad, no more adventures, no more— her throat tightened—*friends.*

"Hurry!" she repeated, pounding the lion's head knocker.

"I don't know why you are so grumbly these days." Sunny arrived, standing next to her and throwing an arm around Esther. "We're here."

Yeah, but for how long?

Vee and Aneta joined them. The door opened. Beverly Beake smiled at them, opening the door all the way. "Do come in, girls. Lovely to see you, as always." She pushed her glasses up on her nose. "Byron is out puttering around in the back somewhere."

They passed through the foyer, with the dining room and sitting room on either side. They passed the kitchen and the breakfasting room, stepped out the french doors, and were surprised to see Byron patching another flight-pen screen. The girls shot a look at each other and hastened to him.

"Sabotage?" Esther asked, knowing it was. She thought of the goggles they had brought. No practice run. The Squad *had* to prowl tonight because the chicken farmer had struck again. Maybe they'd even catch him tonight, but only if they persuaded their parents and the Beakes to allow them to remain on the estate.

His lips pressed in a fine line, Byron nodded. "Blighters."

"Blighters," Aneta repeated. "Blighters. Blighters are not good people?"

"People doing bad things." He was distracted, working on the patch.

"Mr. Beake," Esther began.

Byron cut her off. "I've done the feeding." He smiled a small smile at Esther to show he wasn't mad. "You'll not need to slingshot the food to Howard today."

They had taken too long in Bill's garage. With Vee next to her, Esther glowered up at her taller friend. "I knew we'd taken too much time playing in those dumb boxes."

Vee stepped away, hurt then anger flaring in her dark eyes. The Vee Stare in full force.

I don't care. She's not the boss of me.

Vee spit out the words through her clenched teeth. "Sorry. That's only where we found the night-vision goggles that *my* stepdad is *letting* us use to—"

"Mr. Beake!" Aneta's voice cut through the escalating *uh-oh* between Vee and Esther. "We want to play with the night-vision goggles that Vee's stepdad, Bill, is letting us use. May we stay after dark?" She linked arms with Esther and Vee. "We are the Squad, and we want to do it together."

Aneta never liked anyone to be angry.

Sunny spun. "Yeah, guys, except we forgot to ask any of our parents if they would pick us up."

Esther sucked in a quick breath. She, of all people, should not have forgotten. She'd already put her mother on the spot once. Twice was not going to happen in the Martin family. Well, not and have Internet privileges before she turned sixteen. It had been so exciting to see Sunny pull those goggles out of the box, recognize what they were, and know they now had the tools to catch the chicken farmer in the act of sabotaging the flight pens. Then they'd called for permission to head for the estate on their bikes since the rain had lessened to the now-usual mist. Siddy had been yelling something behind Mom on the phone. Could anyone blame Esther for not remembering to ask about staying past dark? Her back teeth closed, and her jaw stiffened. Siddy ruined so many things.

"I'll do one up on you," came Beverly's cheerful voice from behind the group. Byron and the girls turned as one. The Bird Lady approached in her customary waxed navy barn coat. Beads of rain collected from the mist and popped up when it hit the waxy surface. Esther desperately wanted a coat like that. It looked like Beverly was headed toward adventure whenever she wore it. Probably, though, with where Esther was moving, it would never rain and she'd never get the coat.

Putting a warm hand on Esther's shoulder, Beverly continued, "Do stay for dinner. I'm cooking a roast anyway. We'll do two veg and some mash. I'll invite your families. It will be one less dinner for your parents to cook. It shall be a grand dinner!"

That was easy. Esther stood a little straighter. "Is there anything we can do to help until it's dark?"

Beverly seemed to think for a moment. "No, but Byron, wouldn't the girls love another peek at the owls on the camera?"

Byron agreed.

They followed Byron to the carriage house in what Beverly called their higgledy-piggledy line. Shushing each other so as not to scare Bubo and the second owl, they made their way to the large, covered pen. At the back stood the long table with the computer and an oversized monitor. Byron clicked a couple of places and then the two owls, larger on the screen than they really were in life, were looking right at them. Suddenly, Esther was again glad she hadn't cheated.

"Whoa!" Sunny said, stepping back.

"They are looking right at us!" Aneta said, stepping forward for a closer look. "Do they know we are here?"

Bubo's buddy sidestepped over to Bubo and dug his head under Bubo's wing.

"Aww," said the girls.

"Oh yes," Byron said emphatically. "They heard you a lot earlier than when we opened the carriage house door. Their hearing is superb."

"Maybe they're getting used to us," Vee said.

He fiddled with the zoom on the keyboard. "Let's hope not."

Esther felt her face warming, even though the carriage house was cool. Her secret naming of the smaller of the two—the one she was convinced would stay and be a teaching bird—was still safe. She'd told no one about Bubo. And she hadn't cheated.

"Oh, right," Vee spoke quickly.

"Yeah, we don't want them to become imprinted on humans," Sunny chimed in, her words so close on the heels of Vee's that the other girl frowned at her.

"Oh," was Aneta's reply, her face pinking.

Hmm. Did they share a secret? Again the left-out feeling crowded into the joy of watching the two teenaged owls move about the pen.

Bubo was finishing his dinner. Esther couldn't say she was over the whole mouse thing, but at least now she had a quick reminder to herself that it was just dinner and God created animals to eat each other. Bubo and his sister or brother—Beake Man said it often took a blood test to tell the sex of an owl—wobbled around.

Seemed as though his wings were open more today. She hoped so. She couldn't wait for him to be better. Maybe Beverly would let her go with her and help somehow when Bubo became an education owl.

Chapter 18

In the Dark

When the Squad whispered good-bye to the owls and tiptoed out, deep twilight had dropped over the trees, with the outline of the old Victorian against an only slighter paler sky. Time for goggles.

Byron waved good-bye and headed to the house, where he said he would attempt to get some peace and quiet before "the dinner event." Esther assured him they would be no bother.

"Of course," Sunny said after Byron was out of earshot, "we've told Frank that before, too."

Esther hurried to the back of the house where they'd dumped their backpacks. Looping straps over both arms, she handed them out.

"Okay, so the first thing is put them over your head like this." She placed the googly eyepieces over her own eyes and lifted the straps up and over her head.

"Or not," Vee said, inspecting her unit. She pulled hers on, pulled a strap here and there.

"You look like a space alien." Aneta sounded less and less like the Ukrainian orphan she'd been almost two years ago.

Wearing her goggles, Sunny walked toward Aneta with stiff legs and arms outstretched. "I am gonna get chew," came her muffled tones through the mask. Aneta shrieked and backed away, laughing.

"Okay, we need to try them out." If Esther didn't get bossy, they would all just play. This was *serious*. "First, let's find out what we can see with them on. Be sure to turn them on." Esther's hand trembled as she tightened the straps. Finally! They were getting somewhere! With these, they would be able to see footprints in the mud in the dark, and who knew what else? Maybe the chicken farmer would think he was so clever and simply walk into the Beake woods while the girls wore the goggles. It could happen.

Bill had given Vee the responsibility to hang on to the goggles for a week. *Lord, it would be great to have it all over tonight.* All the families would be there to cheer the Squad and celebrate.

With twilight faded to true night, the girls switched on their goggles.

"Cool," Vee said, rocking a center switch on hers. "I can see a lot better with this switch."

"Bill is the coolest." Sunny fiddled with her mask.

Looking up from arranging her own mask, Esther saw the red dot of light coming from Vee's mask. "Turn that off!" she yelped, scurrying and thumping the rocker switch that sat across Vee's nose.

"Ow!" Vee stepped back and promptly ran into Aneta, who stood behind her muttering about whether she had the right end up on her face.

"Ow!" Aneta echoed, ripping off her mask and also rubbing her nose. "Vee, you bumped my nose very much!"

"Well, Esther practically punched me in the nose. What did you *do* that for, Esther?" Vee's voice was surprised, hurt.

All Esther could see were three lumpy goggles making her friends look like strange frogs from another planet. She wanted to snicker a bit, but when things were drastic, you couldn't fool around. "C'mon, Vee. Because that switch shows right where you are. Bill told us in the garage. The chicken farmer would see you right away."

Sunny, who had pulled on hers first and was darting around in the dark, crouching low and hiding behind trees, sidled up beside the other three. "Esther. We are practicing. We are not expecting to see that Awful Person. I mean, really, what would we do if we saw him? He probably still has his gun with him. All the night-vision goggles would do is show us the gun, and that's not something I want to see better in the dark. In fact, I wouldn't be seeing it 'cause I'd be running as fast as I could and using the goggles not to smack into any trees on my way to the house!"

Esther had tried to be patient, but now her hands fisted and planted themselves on her hips. She spoke very slowly. "We have to find final evidence that the chicken farmer is the one who slingshotted our owls. And all you guys want to do is complain!" Didn't they see the importance? Vee not paying attention and playing around with something that could cause Big Trouble, as Sunny would say? The knot inside gave a tremendous pinch. Words she hadn't planned on saying out loud spurted out of her mouth like, well, her lunch the day she tried to chop a mouse. "You all don't care! You don't care about our owls! Well, fine! I'll just do it by myself!"

She pushed past Sunny who had stopped spinning and was staring at her with her mouth like an *O*. Vee's brows slammed together. Aneta, who had put her mask back on, gave her an alien glance with blank black eyes, mouth turned down.

She would show them. She would find the last, best evidence. Then the girls would know how much the Squad meant to her, how she deserved to have a place in it. Then maybe, just maybe, they would miss her when she was—her lips quivered as she stomped into the trees past the flight cages—*gone*.

The moment she was on the far side of the cages, the quiet surrounded her like a big tent. It was strange to think that she "heard" quiet, but that's what it was. With just her and the trees close together, the girls seemed a million miles away.

"And that's what they will be when I'm gone. Might as well be a million miles away." She heaved a big sigh that seemed to stick in her throat. *Look for clues.* If she could at least find the evidence for their last Squad mission. . .

After a few futile moments of circling trees, slowly raising the goggles up and down, backtracking to closely check the pens—apologizing to the occupants for disturbing them—Esther began to wonder. Why weren't the girls coming after her?

It was a dumb question.

She was all alone because she'd made them hate her. *I was mean. I was bossy.* They liked Melissa better because she's rich and acted nicey-nice to them. The weight of these thoughts bogged her down so much she sagged against the nearest pine tree and slid down to the ground until the bush in front covered her. Sure, the bark scraped her back, but who cared?

A big bubble of a sob was building up in her throat, and in a minute it was going to gush out really loud. She swallowed. *Don't.* Hunching her knees to her chest, she swung her glance back and forth in the goggles. Everything was shades of green and deeper green. Trees, trees, trees. Trees had been getting in her way this whole project.

On the last sweep—as she lifted her hand to yank off the goggles and toss them down—a glow of red eyes froze her solid. Low to the ground. A wolf? Too low. The dull red gaze moved in and out, about the distance of two Byrons lying down end to end. It was headed toward her. A shiver rushed down her spine. What was it? When she heard a chirp, she let out the breath she didn't realize she had been holding. A small critter, a chipmunk or mouse or squirrel. Nothing to be afraid of.

Snap!

A chippy would never snap a branch. The six feet of the S.A.V.E. Squad girls, including a spinning Sunny, would never make a single *snap* sound. Esther oh so carefully pushed the goggles into the bush, parting the branches with her face.

I've got him was the first triumphant thought. *Wait till the girls see me bring back that Awful Person.*

Immediately following that thought came the what-ifs. What if she grabbed him and he got away? Without the girls to help her— what if he yanked free of her death grip and disappeared into the woods? Nobody would believe she'd really had him. The girls would though, wouldn't they? Her prickly, angry words that had singed them all throughout this mission made her want to cry and punch something. What if they were sick of her being bossy and prickly? What if they *didn't* believe her?

A shadowy, lighter green figure with white streaks near the feet— must be shoelaces—emerged from a thicket and began a hunched-over approach. The nearest flight cage—Howard's cage. She blinked twice to make sure she was seeing what she thought she was seeing then squeezed her eyes shut. A long green something, sort of like a wishbone, hung from one hand. What kind of gun looked like a wishbone?

Esther silently breathed in and out like she imagined a spy would. Opening her eyes, a second observation through the eyepieces choked the next breath. Now the figure had straightened and was looking around. Had he—wait, now—had he heard Esther *breathing*? No, she knew she was hidden within the bush.

Wait a sec.

The figure was too short even for the short chicken farmer, with long hair and a way of tossing the head.

Realization washed over Esther in a hot wave that made her forget her right leg was dead asleep. That long thing the person was carrying was a thing to cut the locks off the cages. She'd seen one in school when someone had forgotten their combination. Even worse, she now knew the Squad had been terribly wrong about who used the slingshot on the owls and tore the screens.

That shadowy greenish-white image in the night-vision goggles was not that Awful Person the chicken farmer.

That Awful Person was Melissa.

Crash! Crash!

"Esther! Don't be mad! Where are you?" Aneta's voice soared through the trees. Melissa's goggled head jerked up toward the sound.

No, not now! Esther screamed in her head at the girls, for after Aneta's voice was Sunny's with, "For pizza sake, Esther, if you wanted us to follow you, you at least should have told us." Those two came into view in Esther's goggles with Vee behind, her mask swinging from her hand. What was she thinking? How was she going to see Melissa with no mask?

Whipping her head back to where Melissa stood, Esther's heart collapsed.

The woods were empty.

Chapter 19

All Is Lost

I'm telling you, it was Melissa," Esther was explaining as fast as she was walking back to the house. Her breaths came in little gasps. "She was as tall as Melissa, has long hair, and flipped it just like Melissa does. No way was it the chicken farmer."

"We're going to be late for dinner. Walk faster, Esther." Vee was several steps ahead. Esther didn't think she was even listening.

I found the person who hurt the owls! Who did the sabotage! She couldn't wait until the Squad told Byron.

"But why Melissa, Esther?" Aneta's long legs had no trouble keeping up with everyone.

With a sigh of exasperation, Esther repeated what she'd been telling the girls since the first day Melissa offered to help and suggested maybe Esther wasn't up to being a S.A.V.E. Squad member anymore.

"I don't know about that. Maybe someone who looks like Melissa?" Sunny sounded unsure.

They passed the carriage house and broke into a group trot. With the breakfasting room dimly lit with only a lantern-like lamp, Esther assumed dinner must be in the dining room at the front of the house.

The girls always had their "nibbles," as the Bird Lady called their snacks, on the back stairs that cascaded from the back door outside the breakfasting room.

"Why didn't you guys come and help me?" This came out rougher than she had wanted it to. But really, why hadn't they?

"Look." Vee swung around and faced her, forcing Esther to jerk to a stop. They were on the side of the house. "Sunny convinced us you were setting up some silly training. When you didn't come back by the time the Bird Lady came out to tell us dinner was ready and *our parents are here*, we went to find you. End of story." Vee flounced off around the corner.

Esther heard her footsteps on the front steps and the front door open and slam shut.

Well.

When she, Sunny, and Aneta stepped through the door, Esther looked at both of them. "You believe me, don't you? I saw Melissa. She's the one."

Sunny slid a look toward Aneta who looked unhappy then swung her gaze back to Esther. "Maybe you should keep it quiet for a while about what you saw. I mean, night-vision goggles aren't like what we see in real life."

Aneta nodded, her blue eyes full of tears.

They didn't believe her. Her own beloved Squad didn't believe her.

"Fine. I'll go tell everyone else. *They'll* believe me."

Brushing past them before they could reply, she turned sharply into the dining room. Vee's mom and Bill sat at the long table set with a roast, bowls of mashed potatoes, and vegetables. The tablecloth—a real one—reflected so much white from the chandelier it made Esther's eyes blink after being in the dark. Sunny's parents were there, without her brothers. Esther's eyes widened when she saw Aneta's mom sitting next to Sunny's uncle Dave.

"Esther! Esther! Esther is home!"

Siddy. Her little brother struggled to remove himself from her father's lap. "Here we are! Here we are!"

Her heart dropped to her muddy toes. How could her parents? He would go on with that for all of dinner. Her glare flew to her mother, but it was rebuffed by Mom's upraised eyebrows.

Feeling both the girls standing behind her and the heat shooting up the back of her neck, Esther raised her hands to shush her brother. "Shh, Siddy. Time to be quiet."

"Time to be quiet! Time to be quiet!"

Maybe once the girls sat down, Siddy would quiet down. She dropped into the nearest chair, by Byron. Sunny, Aneta, and Vee found seats. Beverly nodded to her brother, and he prayed over the meal. How come his English accent made the meal blessing sound so much cooler?

As soon as the amens faded away—Dad had, Esther noticed, covered Siddy's mouth during the blessing—the conversation broke out all over the table. Frowning, Esther took this in. She was going to have to be a bit bossy here—for everyone's good, and especially for the Squad.

"I found who shot the owls." Even to her, her voice was louder than usual.

It did, however, create the desired effect. All conversations ceased. She had every eye upon her. Good.

"Vee, what have you girls been up to?"

"Aneta, honey, what's going on?"

"Sunny! Did you forget to fill us in on something?"

The three girls swiveled their gazes to Esther. Sunny drew her lips down in a horrific *what-are-you-doing* face. Aneta pinked up and began to stammer, "I do not—well—I did not." Vee gathered the worst Vee Stare ever and shot it full-force at Esther.

Esther burst out, "It was me who found her. She hurt the owls! She was going to get the Squad in trouble. I saw her in the woods. It's not the chicken farmer."

Parents murmured, "Who's *she*?"

Siddy perked up. "She did it! She did it!" he bellowed, slipping out of his father's lap like a greased pig at a carnival and running toward Esther. She knelt to grab him, but he eluded her and made a circuit of the table, shouting the phrase in his high-pitched and majorly practiced vocal cords.

"Siddy!" Esther shouted. "Sit down and be quiet!"

Siddy didn't sit and wasn't quiet.

"Esther," her mom said.

The parents' murmurs got louder. Beverly looked around from her place at one end of the table. Byron sat in his chair, ramrod straight, the overhead chandelier highlighting his wispy hairs.

They weren't getting it.

"I know who slingshotted our owls. It was Melissa. She's the one who's been messing with the cages, too." She directed this sentence to Byron, who did not respond. "I saw her in the woods." With a nod toward Bill, whose eyes were wide as he watched Siddy who was continuing to yell, she pronounced, "With your night-vision goggles."

Byron cleared his throat. "I think—"

At the same moment, Esther's dad said, "Esther, please sit down. Siddy, be quiet!"

"She did it! She did it!" Siddy was ecstatic. He hadn't had a phrase like this in a long while. Then, to Esther's horror, her little brother remembered another favorite phrase: "We're moving! We're moving!"

The girls gasped, turning to their friend who now had no words to say. "What?"

The table was now a complete mess, people asking her parents about moving, the Squad running up to her and asking questions—mostly, "Why didn't you tell us?"—and Siddy still shouting, voice shooting higher and shriller. "We're moving!"

If only he could stop. Why didn't her parents just make him stop? His repeating was wrecking everything.

"Shut up, Siddy!" Esther roared. "You're ruining everything! *You always ruin everything.*"

Siddy stopped running, stopped hollering. He clasped his small hands in front of him and hunched his shoulders, big eyes wide and clear until a tear slipped out of each one.

Chapter 20

Regrets

She would be in eighth grade before she ever got on the Internet again. Two weeks after she'd hurt her brother so terribly, she was still grounded from the computer. Esther rolled right, then left on her bed, then right again. It was only Monday and still two hours till dinner.

Siddy was staying away from her like he expected her to smack him. Her parents had talked with her about being disappointed and how mean she'd been to her brother and then about Melissa and how you can't accuse people without proof.

Yes, she was sorry she'd hurt Siddy. So very sorry. About Melissa? With being grounded and the girls not speaking to her, hard evidence was out of her reach. If that wasn't bad enough, Byron had shut them out for good this time. She sat up, leaned forward to find her slippers, and, like she was plodding through chocolate pudding, began to pick up her room.

That night, when her mouth shot off without her brain attached, Byron had stood suddenly and said, "This isn't going to work. You must all go home and not return. Please." He didn't sound mad, but he did sound like he meant it. Then he'd done what he hadn't since the first afternoon the girls had met him. He turned and left the room. The sound of the back door shutting followed soon after.

The party was over.

Well.

So now her secret was out. The Squad knew she was moving. The trouble was, she'd been such a bossy brat, they didn't care anymore. Not a single one had called to ask if she'd lost her mind. Well, she had lost, lost it all—helping the owls, watching the wild one get launched back, maybe getting to do the launching. And the S.A.V.E. Squad. The tears that had been so hot and burning for fourteen days seared their way out of her eyes again. She was so tired of crying.

It isn't fair.

When she got to this part, the tears dried up and she got mad. It was Melissa's fault. If Melissa hadn't hurt the owls, tried to weasel her way into the Squad, and then tried to make them look bad with the sabotage, none of this would have happened.

Yes.

It was all Melissa's fault. The stuck-up rich girl who always got what she wanted.

"Esther." Her mom came into Esther's bedroom, her gaze quickly traveling around the neatly made bed, the clear floor, and the desk without piles. "Your room looks great, honey."

Esther shrugged.

"I'm going to run some errands. I'd like you to come with me."

"Who's going to watch Siddy?" Usually when her mother did errands, Esther got stuck at home babysitting Siddy, since Toby couldn't make him mind.

"We'll leave him with your dad at the church. We'll just hurry, since your dad has appointments later this afternoon before he can come home for dinner."

Now they didn't trust her to watch her own brother. She sighed and headed for the garage and the minivan. How to get back into the Squad? She didn't know, and this was nothing the Internet could tell her. If she were *allowed* on the Internet.

At the church, they dropped off Siddy. He ran toward her dad's open arms yelling what her father said to the congregation every Sunday: "This is the day that the Lord has made!" Siddy was sweet, and she had been mean. Double sigh.

Esther's mom drove to Snipp's Super Saver where the two split up the grocery list. While Esther was grabbing items on the list, dumping them in the basket and crossing them off, she was rummaging through her mind. How to get back into the Squad? How to catch Melissa? How to make it right with Siddy? What would Imogene do?

Yeah right. She must be clean out of ideas if she was wondering what a book character would do.

Soon the last item on the To Do list was to drop off a bunch of books at the library, leaving Esther no closer to answering the boiling questions in her head. She slumped in her seat. She couldn't wait to hide in her room again.

"We'll have to go in instead of use the book drop," Mom said, the minivan rolling down Main Street toward the turn for the library. "Siddy needs more Imogene books."

That Imogene. Her little brother, odd and exuberant, adored Imogene. He thought she was smart. He trusted her. He thought she was beautiful, although the illustrations of the gap-toothed, wild-haired amateur detective indicated otherwise. Esther found herself wishing she were Imogene.

"Mom." An idea rose to the top of the turmoil. "Can I get the *Hey, Imogenes*? I want to read to Siddy. He likes Imogene. Maybe he'll like me again if I read to him."

"Oh, honey," her mother said, reaching a hand from the steering wheel to squeeze Esther's knee. "He loves you so much. He's just confused now because. . .well, because of a lot of things." She sighed a deep sigh like Esther had been doing for two weeks. "It's not easy being Siddy." Returning her hand to the steering wheel, she put on her right blinker. "But that would be great if you could get the next batch. I don't know what I'm going to do when he gets through the series."

With her little brother being the lovey-dovey boy he was, Esther was certain the *Hey, Imogene!* books would restore their closeness. Now. About the Squad. *What can I do to get back into the Squad?* What could she do for them to show she was sorry for being so bossy?

As her mother turned off Main, passing The Sweet Stuff, Esther shot to attention like she'd been pinched. Hard.

The S.A.V.E. Squad minus one were walking out of the ice cream parlor.

With Melissa.

"I feel worse. How could I feel worse? I might as well move now." Esther, clutching the next four *Hey, Imogene!* books, regarded Nadine with puppy eyes. She hated it when Siddy drooped puppy eyes at her, but there she was, practically bawling in front of the children's librarian.

Nadine brushed her bangs out of her eyes. She smiled. Two things happened when Nadine smiled. Her whole face lifted up like it was happy to have a smile on it, and she didn't look like a scary librarian who hated kids. "Esther, sometimes things aren't really what we see."

Her parents were forever telling her that. "What does that *mean*?

I don't get it." She gulped. "The girls hate me, and Melissa is getting away with hurting owls and taking my place in the Squad."

Nadine's smile stretched farther as she glanced over Esther's shoulder. "Maybe this will help. What you see is the girls hate you, and you don't know how to make them not hate you."

"Right."

Finally. Someone was *getting* it.

"I think that maybe what you see is not the truth of the way it really is."

Not again! Esther opened her mouth, but Nadine held up an index finger.

"I *see* you're wrong. Turn around."

Rolling her eyes and shaking her head, Esther obediently turned. Sunny, Aneta, and Vee were charging across the library toward her, arms out, shrieking in whispers, "Esther! You're here! You're here!" A breath later, she was swarmed by Squaders and everyone was laughing and crying, including Nadine.

Chapter 21

Now What?

The next day, back to Squad familiar territory, Vee said, "You're crazy, girl." Vee crumpled her face into a can't-believe-it look. "You thought we hated you?"

"I love you, Esther." Aneta hugged her for the bazillionth time.

Even with the four of them sitting in their customary place between two aisles of bookshelves behind Nadine's chair, Sunny managed to spin on her rear end and throw her arms in the air. "We were investigating what you said about Melissa."

Esther blew out a breath. Now she was crying because she was happy. Her cheeks felt stiff with the dried tears. "I'm sorry I was bossy and pushy and—"

Vee interrupted, and for once Esther didn't mind. "Now we know why you were. 'Cause you were, you know."

With a sheepish grin, Esther nodded. "I was."

"You wanted one last perfect Squad mission before you have to move, which I want to tell you I am majorly bummed about," Sunny said, looking at Esther upside down from where she sprawled.

"I think I will hide you in my closet," Aneta said with another hug.

"What if we each buy a really big suitcase and move with Esther?" Sunny suggested.

"I'm going to ask my dad for some of his frequent flier miles so we can go see you!" Vee, as always, the practical one.

An unsteady sigh left Esther. She was still a S.A.V.E. Squad girl.

"I was afraid once you found out I had to move, you would let Melissa take my place. And then I thought she would get my place before I left!"

"No way." Sunny shook her cloud of red curls.

"But sometimes when I mentioned Melissa, you would look at Vee and then you guys wouldn't say anything. And then I saw you guys with her yesterday at The Sweet Stuff!" Esther still needed facts.

Sunny looked at Aneta, who looked at Vee, who leaned forward and glanced at Sunny.

"You mean the looks when we were walking to the edge of the forest—right before we had to climb trees fast?"

Esther nodded.

"Sunny and I had been asking Beverly why you were so grumpy and what had we done. She said we needed to talk to you, but—"

"I was too grumpy."

"Right."

"Okay, I'll tell the rest." Sunny leaned back on her hands. "We didn't believe you when you first said you saw Melissa through the night-vision goggles."

Esther raised her eyebrows.

"I know." Sunny leaned on her right hand and waved Esther's expression away with her left. "Afterward, we talked. None of us wanted to lie and say we believed you if we didn't."

"But you ran out to the van before we could tell you," Aneta supplied.

Great.

Vee walked up and down before them. "We agreed we needed to investigate."

"'Cept we could never find Melissa until just before we were coming here." Sunny jumped up and walked behind Vee, imitating her stride. She told Esther that when they saw Melissa and her driver parked at The Sweet Stuff, they knew it might be their only chance, so they followed her in.

"We were coming to see Nadine to see how to get you to be with us again. We figured you were grounded from the Internet, not us."

So. Esther had seen them after their interrogation at The Sweet Stuff.

"The S.A.V.E. Squad rocks!" Esther clapped her hands. "Did you get her to confess?"

Another trading of back-and-forth looks. Sunny, nominated by nods, spoke. "Nope."

No? Esther's brows nearly touched each other with her frown. If she'd been there—but wait, bossy had separated her unnecessarily from the Squad already. She wasn't going there again.

"She has an alibi." Aneta pronounced the word carefully.

"She can't! I *saw* her!" Esther wanted to grab her hair and yank. Not Aneta's long, blond ponytail. Hers. She *knew* she'd seen her. A tiny doubt prickled her scalp. Hadn't she?

Vee shook her head. "Now we are sure. You didn't see her."

"Why didn't I?"

They pointed to the large meeting room just off the entrance to the library and said together, "She was there."

When Esther still didn't understand, Sunny told her that Melissa had been giving a PowerPoint presentation—of course—about her horse school in France.

"On our way in, we checked with the front desk. The lady there said it was supposed to be a picture slideshow of France, but it was all Melissa—of course. Melissa jumping horses, Melissa eating some incredible pastry, Melissa jumping another horse, Melissa standing in her riding gear, Melissa—"

"Okay!" Esther interrupted. "I get it." She threw out her hands in a gesture of *now what?* "I was so sure." This was not great news. It meant she'd dumped some major drama on a whole lot of people. And been wrong. Esther hated being wrong. As the oldest, she was right more than she was wrong. With the Squad, sometimes they didn't listen to her enough to know she was right. Boy, she'd been wrong big-time this time. "So now everybody at the dinner thinks Melissa did it. Great. Just great." A big blast of air burst from her, and she fell flat back on the carpet. "What do I do now?"

"You mean what do *we* do now. We're the Squad, right?"

"Why the worried faces, my chicks?" The Bird Lady stood over Esther and smiled down at her then around at the group.

"We're in Big Trouble." Sunny leaped to her feet. "We found out Melissa didn't do the sabotage, and now Beake Man thinks we're trouble and we'll never get back to help the owls so we can see them launch back to the wild."

Vee jerked her thumb toward redheaded Sunny. "Pretty much what she said."

Esther struggled to her feet. "Plus I have to apologize to everyone at your house for yelling that Melissa was the one messing with the flight pens." *Might as well get started with the sorrys.* "I'm sorry I ruined your dinner. I'm sorry I was pushy and bossy and said stuff that wasn't true. I'm sorry Byron now thinks we're just like all the other kids." Her voice trailed off with another gusty sigh. All this apologizing was tough.

Wrapping a skinny arm around Esther, Beverly Beake pulled her to her side. "Oh, child. We will all survive you making a mistake. And you are quite wrong about Byron thinking you're trouble."

"We are?" the Squad said.

Beverly nodded and waved to Nadine, who was returning to her desk. "Oh yes, indeed. The sabotage and Esther seeing someone on the property that night made him worried for you girls' safety."

"Then why did he get all mad and yell?" Esther wanted to know.

"I know!" Aneta, who had been listening with brow furrowed, brightened and raised her hand like she was in school. "He was like Esther at dinner!"

What?

Her friend turned to her, excited at her understanding of this English language. "Yes! You wanted very much to find who shot the owls. Little brother would not be quiet. You yelled to make us listen because you wanted this very much."

Heat crept up Esther's neck as Sunny and Vee snorted with laughter. Nadine and the Bird Lady pressed their lips together.

Okay.

"I get it," she said, making a hideous face at the floor. "He wanted us to be safe. To make sure we wouldn't come back. He was mad at the sabotage, not us." When she looked up, she asked the Bird Lady, "But how do we get back into the estate to help with the birds? How do we find the slingshotter so all Byron's birds are safe?"

Beverly's face lifted in a smile. "I can't wait to see what you girls come up with for *that*."

The two women waved good-bye and left for their lunch date.

"Whoa, you *guys*!" Sunny clutched her hair as soon as they were out of earshot.

"What?" Vee looked startled at Sunny's outburst. She'd been looking at her Anti-Trouble Phone, or the ATP, as the girls called it.

Sunny hopped up and down, hands still in her hair. "Esther is *moving*. We've *got* to solve this case!"

Chapter 22

What Would Imogene Do?

When Sunny began wriggling and squirming, the girls declared they needed to go outside and exercise Sunny before one of the other librarians tossed them out. The rain had stopped and the sun was out, at least for now, so they left their raincoats piled under Nadine's chair. After a few steps of trying to keep pace with the other girls as they walked through the parking lot, Esther pulled off her sweatshirt and tied it around her waist. It felt good to do Squad things again.

The Squad needed ideas on how to get back to the estate, and they needed them now. The birds had been doing so well the last time they'd seen them; the girls told each other it would be any day now. The launch back to the wild! They would miss it. *It's not fair.* Esther snorted and told herself to chill. A lot of things weren't fair. Like moving away from the best friends on the planet. . .

Sunny was still bouncing and darting around each of the girls. *Just like Siddy. Can't sit still.*

"Okay Sunny, you and Vee race to the end of the pavement and back. Go!" Esther said.

The two girls took off. It was no contest. Vee was back and not even breathing hard before Sunny reached the end of the pavement; the redhead laughed and skipped her way back. "That felt good. All this rain makes me feel like I'm building up steam and I'm gonna *blow*!"

Esther glanced back over at the Dumpster in the community center parking lot. Near it stood a bushy pine tree with two odd white blocks tucked under it. The Squad knew what those cubes were. That had been their second adventure. A couple of the community cats sat on the closed Dumpster. Was the black-tailed Flick from the Great Cat Caper there?

"Remember—" She pointed. The girls followed the direction of her pointing finger. "That was a crazy adventure."

Vee rubbed her knee. "Boy, do I."

"A great adventure, although it sure didn't seem like it was going to be." Sunny spun around and around, barely landing on the ground before she twirled again.

"Frank and Nadine were so angry," Aneta remembered.

They kept walking.

"Remember the first time we met each other. . . ," Sunny said, walking backward in front of them.

"Don't do that, Sunny, you'll fall and break your head." Esther took in a deep breath. Remembering was fun, and it was sad. If she took deep breaths and didn't actually look at the girls, maybe she wouldn't cry.

"Yeah, and some of us did not pay attention, and some of us were bossy, and some of us did not want to be there." Aneta shivered. "I was so afraid."

"Ole Frank still says we are drama girls." Sunny's smile showed she didn't believe him.

"An idea!" Aneta squealed, stopping and clasping her hands as though holding her thought. "Why do not we do with Byron Beake what we do with Frank?"

"Push his buttons and make him mad?" Sunny asked.

"No," Aneta spoke through her chuckle. "Tell him we know we were not doing it right and say we are sorry."

The other three considered this, reaching the lake. Sunny roamed the beach looking for rocks to skip. When no one spoke, Aneta said, "It is not a good idea?"

"It is, Aneta." Vee patted her friend's shoulder. " 'Cept we already did that with Byron, remember?"

"Yeah," called Sunny from the beach where she was as close to the water as she could get and not get wet feet. "When we thought he was a kidnapper." She bounced up and down. "Okay, guys, what about this? This could be the rocko-socko Great Idea we need! Okay, here's the deal." Sunny came up from the water's edge, gathered the girls in, and lowered her voice. "We don't ask for Byron to let us in. We go to the gate and say we're there to see Howard."

"Howard?" Vee looked incredulous.

"Yeah, yeah." Sunny's blue eyes widened. "We make a super treat for Howard and tell Byron he has to let us in because we are not staying, only bringing Howard his treat. Then when we get in there, Byron will see that we are totally safe and voilà!" Sunny leaped into the air and turned in a circle. "Tada!"

Three blank faces regarded her. Then Aneta turned her head toward Vee. Vee shrugged and looked at Esther. Esther put her hands on her hips. "Sunny, you've been spinning too much. Howard eats *roadkill*. It's not like we can make"—she waved her hand, trying to think of something to show Sunny she was cuckoo—"roadkill *cupcakes* or something!"

Sunny's lip curled, and she made an "ew" sound. "Oh," she said. "Good point."

Vee pulled out her notebook and tiny pen and scribbled. "Two ideas down. So let's think about what Byron wants."

"Us not to come back," Sunny said.

"Sunny, be quiet," Aneta said.

Sunny pressed her lips together, took two fingers, and pretended she was locking her lips and throwing away the key.

"He wants us to be safe. So what if we come with a bodyguard?" Vee looked up from her scribbling.

A bodyguard. Esther thought this was a terrible idea, but she didn't say anything because she didn't want to be bossy with Vee anymore.

"A bodyguard." Sunny squinted at Vee. "Like which of us knows a bodyguard?"

"You mean like a mom or dad?" Aneta asked.

Even worse.

"Bill would be a great bodyguard, but he has to work all the time." Vee pushed the notebook and pen into her back pocket.

"Doesn't that leave C.P.?" Esther said, hoping they would laugh.

They did. It felt good to laugh, even though they still didn't have an answer. They walked out on the dock.

"Remember. . . ," Esther began.

"Yes!" Aneta shivered.

"I'll never forget that day," Sunny said, collapsing on the wooden planks of the dock.

"Crazy," agreed Vee.

Another S.A.V.E. Squad adventure. Their first. When they didn't even like each other.

Remembering that day and all the yelling and screaming and running—especially remembering all the running—Esther was reminded of her little brother. Siddy loved to run and scream. One of Imogene's sayings when she got in trouble for yelling was, "Yelling helps me think."

"What would Imogene say?" she muttered, leaning over her crossed knees and staring into the dark water. Sometimes a bit of sun would catch a ripple just right and it would glow like a silvery snake.

"Who's Imogene?" Vee sat next to her, arms wrapped around her skinny legs. Esther couldn't quite get her arms around her knees, so she dropped her head into her hands, elbows propped on her legs.

"My little brother's favorite book series. It's called *Hey, Imogene!* and he's always hollering out things she says in the books. She's a nine-year-old who's, well, *different*, who solves little kid cases and sometimes big cases by mistake."

"I wish we could solve this case by mistake. At least we would solve it while the four of us are together," Sunny said.

"I'm going to ask to see if you can come for fall break after you move," Vee said suddenly and added ferociously, "I mean it."

"I think. . ." Sunny stood up and looked down at them. "I think we need to go ask the Imogene expert. Right after the library. And Siddy is the expert on Imogene."

"Uhh. . ." Esther's voice disappeared into her surprise. As shown at the dinner, people other than the family—with the exception of C.P., whom Siddy adored—usually got him too excited. Who knew what he'd do?

But Aneta and Vee were already pulling her to her feet and excitedly talking about what they might find out.

"Like what stuff does Imogene say that Sidney yells?" Sunny asked.

" 'Yelling helps me think,' " Esther said quickly.

Vee repeated the words, a frown creasing her brow. "Huh."

"Hey! That works for me!" Sunny shouted, waving her arms.

"And 'Look up when you're down!' " Esther continued.

"I like that one." Aneta smiled.

They were climbing the steps to the library when Esther pulled on Sunny's arm. "Look, you guys. You saw how my brother was at the dinner. He's"—she almost said *weird*, when her love for Siddy swelled up and she finished—"*different.*"

"Ha." Vee leaned against the railing and folded her arms. "The Twin Terrors smell like you can't believe. That's different. And you've only got one Sidney to smell. I've got two." Then her face broke out in a smile. "And a baby soon! I hope it's a girl to even things out."

"My mom says we have *different* relatives she doesn't want me to meet yet," Aneta volunteered.

"Are you kidding? I've been called *different* all my life. What's the big deal?" Sunny trotted up and down the stairs.

Esther remained doubtful, but said, "Okay, just so you know what you're getting yourself into. Vee, can we use the ATP and see if my mom says it's all right and everyone else?"

Vee pulled it from her pocket and handed it to Esther.

As she tapped in her home number and held the phone to her ear, a chill ran up her neck. *If this doesn't work, I might be glad to move.*

Chapter 23

Asking Imogene

*A*n hour later, Esther took in a deep breath and opened the door to her house. The girls crowded in the entryway. Mom appeared at the top of the stairs, a welcoming smile on her face. "Hi, girls!" She pointed to the living room. As the girls settled in the couch and love seat under the soaring cathedral ceilings, Siddy tore down the hall and launched himself at Esther. "Esther is here!"

"That looks familiar," Vee remarked. "The Twin Terrors do that to me all the time."

Esther's mom waved as she headed down the hall. "He loves those *Hey, Imogene!* books. C.P. will be here soon."

"C.P.?" Aneta said. "*Our* C.P.?"

Esther's mother nodded. "Siddy loves him. C.P. comes over and reads *Imogene* books over and over. Sometimes they act out the books in the backyard." She sighed. "It's. . .nice."

It drove Esther crazy to read to Siddy. He had memorized a lot of the books and wouldn't let her skip any words. He had to chant them along with her. The problem was Siddy had no sense of pacing and sped up and slowed down until Esther thought the top of her head would blow off.

Aneta picked up the first one. "*Imogene Tries Out*," she read, opening the wide cover with a full-color drawing of a little girl with a gap-toothed smile, bushy black hair, and glasses with a Band-Aid wrapped around the nose part. She held pom-poms half her size. "Oh, look—Imogene is trying out to be a cheerleader." Aneta turned a page.

The doorbell rang. Siddy ran to the top of the stairs with an armful of books. "Esther's home! Esther's home!"

Esther ruffled the top of his head as she ran down the stairs to let C.P. in. She never should have brought the girls. Finding something helpful about an imaginary kid? From a kid who couldn't communicate? Crazy idea. "Hi, C.P. We need help. We need to know what Imogene says!"

C.P. pushed the last bit of what looked like a peanut butter sandwich into his mouth. C.P. was always eating. "What for? You never cared before." He pushed past her and said to the small boy, "Good to see you. Thanks for coming."

Siddy shifted the books to one hand and head-butted C.P., who seemed to accept this as a usual greeting.

Sidney repeated, "Good to see you. Thanks for coming. Good to see you. Thanks for coming." Relief sounded in the scratchy high voice. He returned to the living room where the girls sat. Aneta and Sunny looked at her brother like he was the coolest thing they'd ever seen. Vee was regarding Siddy intently. *This is a mess.*

Setting down the books, Siddy picked up *Imogene Tries Out.* "Would you like me to read to you, Siddy?"

Esther squatted next to him. Nobody but C.P. knew her brother repeated what people said. Exactly. Someone, some day, had framed that question to Siddy, and now he used it for his way of asking people to read to *him*. This plan today had been *such* a bad idea. Putting her arm around him, she said gently, "No, Siddy." Thinking it through, she began a phrase at a time. What would he repeat? "Esther wants Siddy to tell about Imogene."

Thrusting the book at her, Siddy pranced to an empty chair and patted the empty space next to him. "Would you like me to read to you, Siddy?"

"Why don't you just read it to him?" C.P. looked disgusted. He plopped in the chair with the younger boy and opened to the first page. "Hey, Imogene! Whatcha doing!" he read. Siddy repeated the words in a falsetto voice.

From where she'd flopped on the couch in between Sunny and Aneta, Esther traced a pattern on her jeans. "That's how every story of *Hey, Imogene!* starts."

"Shhh." Aneta put her finger to her lips.

C.P. read *Imogene Tries Out.* Imogene wanted to try out for a cheerleading club. She brought her own pom-poms. The other girls told her they were silly because they were made of tissue paper. She yelled during the practice period. The other girls told her she was too loud. "Yelling helps me think!" she bellowed, pushing at the Band-Aid.

After the first reading, Siddy and C.P. acted out the book. That was pretty funny, and for several minutes, Esther forgot about their goal. The girls left C.P. reading *Imogene Fixes Everything* and thudded down the stairs to Esther's bedroom. Esther was in despair. This whole Imogene thing had been a big nothing.

All four of them flopped across Esther's bed and hung their heads and arms over the side. For a moment, the only sounds were the dishwasher upstairs rumbling the ceiling in Esther's bedroom. Then Aneta raised her hand like she was in school.

"Imogene is different." Aneta's voice was muffled between her hair and the side of the mattress. "Like the Squad."

"She's loud." Sunny began to kick her legs and move her arms like she was swimming. "Like us."

"She doesn't give up." Vee lay perfectly still. "Like us."

"She had great ideas." Esther thought about the tissue paper pom-poms. "Like us."

So what would Imogene do?

Silence.

Oh! "There's always a clue," as Imogene said.

She would think on it overnight.

It could work. They'd be back living the yayness.

"No," Vee said flatly after hearing the plan the next day. "No way." They were in their library place. Nadine was absent from her desk.

"Tissue paper?" Aneta looked like she'd been given a great Christmas present. "That is fun!"

"Be loud? Jump around? I'm in!" Sunny spun and danced her way down the aisle in the stacks and back again.

"Aw, Vee, it's for the birds." Sunny sidled up to the taller girl and slid an arm around her shoulder.

"You got that right. Do I look like a—one of *those*? I don't think so." Vee crossed her arms over her chest.

She had a point. In all their adventures, Esther, Sunny, and even quiet-voiced Aneta yelled. Vee did not yell.

Esther pulled a sorrowful face. "We need four to do it."

Aneta sighed and stuck out her bottom lip. "The S.A.V.E. Squad is so good about taking *opportunities*."

Everyone but Vee thought this was hysterical. It took Esther several minutes to get them back to a serious discussion.

Sunny removed her arm from around Vee and stood over Esther, and Aneta sat on the floor. Chewing on one finger and frowning, the redhead appeared deep in thought. "Yeah, I guess we'll have to ask Melissa to help us."

Vee's choked snort of laughter told Esther everything would be all right.

Chapter 24

Surprise!

On Saturday, Esther awoke before her alarm. Holding her breath, she listened. No patter of raindrops on the patio outside one of her bedroom windows. Her last words before bed had been a prayer that the weather would be, in Sunny words: *rocko-socko* and *complete yayness*. If it rained, it would ruin everything. "Oh thank You, God. You like owls as well as sparrows, don't You?"

After making her bed, taking her dirty clothes down to the laundry room, eating breakfast, and helping Siddy with his, she reported to her mother who was rummaging around in the hall closet.

"Did you find it?"

Her mother emerged, clutching brightly colored material. "Yes! I have several colors, and here's kitchen twine. I think there are only two pairs of scissors in the kitchen desk drawer. Can the girls bring their own?"

Esther called the girls and was reassured that everyone had scissors and they would bring them. Within the hour, the girls arrived and gathered around the dining table.

"I cannot believe I am doing this." Vee looked disgusted, as if the

Squad were making roadkill cupcakes for Howard. Forty-five minutes later, they were finished and rather pleased with themselves—at least Sunny, Aneta, and Esther were. They did a couple of practice runs. Esther's mom thought they were quite funny and said if they pulled that stunt in front of *her* black-iron gate, she would definitely let them in.

"I did call Beverly Beake to let her know you girls would be outside the gate. This way, she'll make Byron go with her on some errand so he'll be outside the fence and see you."

Vee groaned. "He can't miss us." She looked at what she was holding and gushed out a breath. "I'm glad there's not going to be any pictures."

Outside the gate, Aneta turned a face tinged pink with morning chill toward Esther. "I think he is not coming."

"He'll be here. The Bird Lady said she'd make sure." Esther made herself sound confident. What if Beverly couldn't make her brother do what she wanted? That even happened to Esther sometimes.

"Maybe he said no and shut himself in the carriage house." Sunny hopped up and down to warm herself.

"He *better* come if I'm going to look like an idiot for the owls." Vee frowned and adjusted her hair.

Her mom had parked the van under the tree outside the gate where it all started. She stepped out. "You girls can come in. I've got the heat on."

"We don't want to miss being ready, Mom," Esther said.

"But thanks, Mrs. Martin," Vee said.

Esther turned and threw a blazing smile at her mother. "You're the best, Mom. Thanks for driving us and waiting with us."

"This time of year, you never know when it's going to pour, and well, you know that tissue paper. . ."

"Yeah, it would have been toast," Sunny finished for her.

"He's coming!" Aneta sang out. "I see the truck down the road!"

"Go, girls!" Esther's mother called.

They lined up across the gate, making it impossible for the truck to get through without running them over. Esther stepped out of line and inspected her troops. Sunny and Aneta were rustling their pom-poms. Sunny had red, and Aneta had blue.

"I can't believe I'm holding pom-poms." Disdain dripped from each word Vee spit out. She gave each one a shake. Hers were purple. So were the ribbons on her pigtails. That had been a battle.

"You look like a real cheerleader, Vee, except you have to yell loud and smile." Esther sucked in her cheeks so she wouldn't bust out laughing. She punched up with her neon-pink pom-poms. "My mom is a genius, helping us make pom-poms out of tissue paper."

"Closer, closer." Sunny was watching the truck approach.

When it had nearly reached the turn for the driveway, it screeched to a halt.

"Start jumping up and down. The Bird Lady will make him keep coming!" she said, beginning some jumping jacks and waving the pom-poms. Vee muttered something and did a move that made her look like she was cross-country skiing on land. Her pom-poms fluttered in the light breeze that kicked up. The truck turned into the driveway, and the girls were backed against the gate. For a long moment, neither door opened, and then Beverly Beake emerged from the passenger side, looking like she was enjoying a very good joke. Byron remained behind the steering wheel.

Okay. If Byron Beake wasn't coming out, then they would go to him. Esther raised her hands to her hips. The pom-poms rustled. "Follow me!" she cried and trotted to the driver's side of the truck.

Standing about six feet away, she pasted a big smile on her face and shook the pom-poms. The line of Squaders stood straight and looked at Esther expectantly.

The door creaked open, and Byron stepped out. His face behind the mask was smooth, unreadable as always. "What."

This was it. She raised the pom-poms above her head and shouted, "One, two!"

The other three responded with such a roar it startled her. "Three, four!"

Together, with mighty Squad power, they chanted, "Yay, rah, ray!"

Vee, with a considerable shove from Sunny, staggered forward and yelled, "Let us in today!" She backed into line again, her rare smile flashing across her face.

I think she likes this.

Girls: "Yay, rah, ree!"

Aneta pirouetted out, pom-poms high, and hollered, "We'll be safe, you'll see!"

After she darted back, the girls took a collective breath and then shouted, "Yay, rah, reek!"

Sunny, spinning wildly so the pom-poms looked like liquid color, shrieked, "We'll help you, Mr. Beake!"

Byron's mouth was twitching now. He'd come all the way out of the truck and was leaning against the side, arms folded.

Girls: "Yay, rah, rye!"

Esther leaped forward, knelt on one knee, and shook the pom-poms in Byron's direction. "Please let us watch them fly!"

If she said so herself, it was her best bellow ever. Then she hopped back to the line and waited with the girls. Had it worked?

Byron stepped to the front of the truck, grinning at his sister who was chuckling. "Sister, do you want to tell them or should I?"

Chapter 25

Spilled Secrets

Later, Vee sat on the velvet couch in the mansion's living room, shock still evident on her face. "I didn't have to make a fool of myself."

Sunny fell out of the chair, clutching her sides with laughter. "Oh, Vee, if you could have seen your face."

Vee groaned and fell over. The girls were awaiting Beverly bringing snacks. Byron had wandered off after telling them his two big bits of news.

"How would we know that Beake Man woke up this morning and decided the owls were ready to be tested and thought we should be there?" Esther wriggled on the largest ottoman she'd ever seen. It was bright red, with tassels on each corner. Siddy could use this for a bed. Happy. She felt happy, even with the corner-of-her-mind sadness that days were slipping away and soon she and her family would be moving. "So the chicken farmer came over and apologized. Huh." No matter what happened with the mystery person in the woods, the Squad would see the owls launch. Together.

Aneta's face was dreamy. "We are going to watch them launch."

"Not necessarily." Esther felt she had to be accurate. "Byron is going to let us watch him examine them and test them for flight and see if one or two of them can do it."

Vee jumped in. "I wish we knew just *what* he apologized *for*. I still say he recognized that slingshot when he snatched it from Esther that day. Was he apologizing for yelling at Byron or the other stuff?"

Esther wanted to stay happy, at least for a bit. "Today, we'll know if Bubo—" The words died in her throat. *Oh no.* From the frozen looks of the girls, she knew she couldn't pretend she had said something else.

"You named one of the birds?" Sunny's mouth hung open, eyes huge.

Aneta's face was pale. "Oh, Esther, you did? Byron told us not to."

Vee shook her head. "Can't believe it."

Great. Just great. Everything had been going so well.

"I—uh—," she began.

The next moment Sunny tackled her off the ottoman with cackles of laughter. "I named mine Socko!" she choked out.

Vee snuck a look at Aneta, who was pressing her mouth in and out. Vee sighed and said, "Oh, all right. Mine's Cat, for those cat-ear tufty things on his head."

"Legs." Aneta's voice was small, her blue eyes dancing. "Like he's wearing fluffy pants." Of the two owls the girls had rescued—and the one Esther had named—one was much smaller with more pronounced leg feathers. His ears tufted high like Vee's kitten.

"Did we—" Vee straightened, a thought dawning in her expression.

"—all name the same bird?" Sunny finished.

They had.

That set them off again.

"Why did you name him Bubo?" Aneta stood by the fireplace

143

now, stretching from side to side.

Esther explained that her Internet research had shown that the scientific name for a Great Horned Owl was *Bubo virginianus.*

More laughter.

"What?" Esther looked from girl to girl.

"That is so you!" Sunny crowed.

"To look that up!" Vee laughed a happy laugh.

"You are so smart," Aneta marveled.

The hot prick of tears zinged Esther's eyes. "I'm going to miss you guys."

While the girls hooted with laughter in the living room, Byron had moved the two real hooters to an empty flight pen that held perches made out of logs to resemble branches and forks of trees. Outside the pen, the girls watched the two on the perch, feathers tight to their bodies. Esther knew, as did the girls, that this meant they were scared at the change. She wondered if she would walk with her arms tight by her sides the first day in her new school. *I know how you feel, Bubo and friend.*

The owl with all the names sidestepped away from the other and hiked up its wings. The girls gasped. In the six weeks since they'd found the two juvenile owls hissing and tucked in on themselves, each of them had grown significantly larger. The wingspan on Bubo was easily three feet. The other owl watched Bubo, twisting its neck around and nearly upside down, big yellow eyes inquisitive.

Esther laughed.

Byron came alongside her.

Glancing at him and the girls, Esther said, "I know they're wild. I know they do creepy stuff like attack crows in their nests at night. I know they grab their prey with two thousand pounds of pressure with those talons, but sometimes they're just *cute.*"

Byron rolled his eyes then narrowed them. He gestured to the larger, not-Bubo owl. "See how that right wing isn't fully extended?"

The girls gathered closer.

"That's not good. That means that the pulley extension inside him with the feet and the wings is compromised."

"What is *compromised*?" Aneta asked.

Vee spoke up. "Messed up. Like when a spy's cover is compromised, he's in trouble."

Aneta nodded.

A funny-odd-not-funny-ha-ha feeling began in Esther's stomach. "Do you mean he can't go free?"

Byron blew out a breath and looked at the four sad faces. "I told you this at the beginning. Remember? I did tell you." He looked back at the house. "Where's Beverly anyway?"

He had, in fact, told them. *"You never know if an injured wild bird will recover,"* he had said. *"Don't name them or get attached to them,"* he had said, *"because they could die or you'll be sad when they leave."* Yep. He had told them all. By the looks on the Squaders' faces, they remembered it all, and it didn't matter. They felt bad that the not-Bubo wouldn't be flying high and hooting at night. Bubo would be leaving. They hadn't planned on that.

Just like her. She'd expected he'd stay—be there when she came back to visit. She didn't like this change.

"Yikes, I thought for sure it would be the—other one who would stay. He just didn't seem to get the idea that he was supposed to be wild." Sunny shoved her hands into her pockets. Esther noticed she'd almost given away her name for Bubo.

"So now the other owl has to be the one to go back to the wild," Aneta spoke up.

"Not necessarily," Esther pointed out. "Neither of them could."

"No way!" Vee wasn't having any of that. "That would mean we failed big-time."

"If I might add something here," Byron said, arms folded in his *listen-to-me* pose, "you have no control over this. The one who has to go will go. That is all there is to it."

"How does Bu—the other one look?" Esther managed to ask. His words stung: *The one who has to go will go. Ouch, Lord.*

Byron eyed Bubo. Standing next to Byron, Esther felt Aneta's hand slip into hers on the right. Turning her head, she smiled at her friend. Sunny stepped to Aneta's side and linked elbows with her. Vee bumped Sunny's shoulder with her own and raised her eyebrows like *I hope.*

Bubo was the one she'd been sure would stay. He'd been so awkward, not attempting to flap his wings and try them out, seemingly happy with a robotic arm feeding him. Even her slingshot food tossing hadn't tempted him. She guessed he'd given up being wild. Or that he thought the Beakes' refuge was good-enough wild.

"I checked him over this morning, before Beverly got me out on the crazy 'errand.' There's nothing to suggest he can't fly. If he doesn't try here in the flight cage after I take out the other owl, we'll try launching him tomorrow night."

Tomorrow night. Would her last project with the Squad end with Bubo staying with the girls? Or would she watch him fly out of her life, like the girls?

Ouch, ouch, ouch.

Her heart hurt.

Chapter 26

Who Is *THAT*?

At Esther's church the next morning during group prayer time, the girls prayed that Bubo would soar. Then, with arms locked around each other, they prayed Esther would soar like Bubo in her new town. Then they cried.

That evening, as soon as it grew dark, cars, SUVs, and a minivan pulled into Uncle Dave's ranch, just up the road from the Beakes'. Esther had her face pressed against the window in the minivan to get her first glimpse of the girls. The oval of short grass made her grin. That grassy spot had been a fun part of one of their adventures.

Sunny, Esther, and Vee spilled from their vehicles, parents joining them after parking the vehicles in the gravel parking circle. "This will make Dave's place even more special," Aneta greeted them, running out the front door. "Mom and I came early for dinner. Tonight is the night!"

Ho, ho. What if Aneta's mom and Sunny's uncle Dave got married and she didn't get to come? She was going to miss so much.

"Here's hoping Cat flies." Vee's face was a mixture of trying to look happy and still worried at the same time.

Sunny dashed from her parents and spun in a circle around the Squad. "You guys, this is it! I hope Socko takes off."

"You mean Legs," Aneta said with a straight face and then burst out laughing.

"Oh no. You must mean *Cat*." Vee played along.

"You mean my good friend Bubo?" Esther's voice joined in the merriment, but her heart wasn't in it.

The Beakes' truck turned off the county road. Kids and parents surged toward the side of the ranch house, which led to the back corral and then the meadow. Byron had decided that since Todd Hudson, the chicken farmer, had come over to apologize, he would reassure the farmer and launch the owl at Uncle Dave's, a big enough distance from the chicken farm to effect a "new" neighborhood and hunting ground. To everyone's surprise, Todd had asked if he could come. "I don't want them around my chickens, but how often do you get to see an owl up close?" Byron had said yes.

Byron instructed them to stay away from the truck while he removed a dog kennel from the truck bed. He told the girls, "There's no guarantee he will stay in this area. Tonight is the night to say good-bye, if you must." Esther knew better than to ask to hold the owl now. Since she'd seen Bubo stretch his wings, she understood wild was wild, and she wasn't nearly big enough.

The questions zipped back and forth inside her head. Did she want Bubo to remember he was wild and love the majesty of the starred night sky? Or did she want him to flap on Byron's arm and go nowhere, so something would remain the same after she left?

"The one who has to go will go. That is all there is to it."

Byron bent toward the latch. "Okay, everyone, stand here. I'll go forward and remove him from the crate. Please, no sudden moves or shouting."

Good thing Siddy wasn't here.

"Wait a sec, Beake Man."

Byron straightened and looked at the Squad.

Vee punched her arm in the air. "Squad bracelets up to the sky!"

Esther shot up her right arm and was joined by Aneta and Sunny. They didn't say a word, and their smiles were a little crooked.

Vee nodded to Byron, and he unclasped the latch.

They held hands and kept their arms high, making sure not to twitch. That had to be hard for Sunny. Watching Byron and holding hands while her arm went numb, Esther saw a red dot several yards off to the right, where the forest came out and met the meadow. She blinked. She *couldn't* have seen that.

With the owl hissing, Byron removed Bubo from the crate.

Esther nudged Vee and gestured with her head toward the red. Vee took one look and whipped her head back to Esther. *Trouble*, she mouthed at her. Esther nodded.

From their bossy fight that terrible night over whether to use the enhanced function on the night-vision goggles, both of them knew that whoever was wearing them had a better view of the group than they had of the person. But the person apparently didn't know they could see the red light.

That red light also made those goggles easier to see Bubo.

Bubo was out and up on Byron's arm, flapping and stretching more with each powerful move. He was beautiful in his wildness.

And as clear a target as the stars were clear on this night.

Byron had asked them not to twitch or be loud. Maybe he would be mad. Maybe it might scare Bubo. Maybe Bubo would be too scared to fly. Maybe all that. But Esther was a S.A.V.E. Squader, and she had to *do* something. She darted in front of Byron and Bubo, screaming, "Watch out!" Byron's face behind his mask morphed from surprise to incredulity. A burning sting hit the back of her neck, and she stumbled and fell, thinking it was strange she smelled lemon.

What had just happened?

She lay sprawled near Byron's feet, gasping.

Everything then rushed in together. Vee yelling, "Beake Man, get Cat down! Esther's been hit!" Aneta screamed, and Sunny ran up to her, calling her name.

Right as the rushing filled her ears, the lemon smell persisting with the sting spreading to each side of her shoulders, she raised her head and blinked. Bubo was looking down at her, round golden eyes reflected in the bright night. *"The one who has to go will go. That is all there is to it."*

He turned his head in that funny way of his and lifted off Byron's arm, gaining higher and higher, stroking up to the stars.

Chapter 27

Case Solved

"*U*nbelievable."

In the sitting room off Uncle Dave's kitchen, lying on the couch, Esther heard Byron Beake's single word amid the confusion. The paramedics wanted to shine a light in her eyes. Her mom and dad kept repeating, "Esther, honey, can you hear us?" The Squad chirped various sentences like, "Tell me you're not dead, Esther," "That was so brave," and "That was pretty stupid, Esther." A less-familiar voice filtered in as well. "I'm so sorry. I had no idea she would. . ." But now the back of her neck was freezing, and wetness was slipping down her back. *Ick.*

She tried to sit up, reaching back to push away the coolness, but hands pressed her down. "I'm not dead," she snapped.

Finally, they let her sit up.

"Who's 'she'?" she demanded, leaning back against the cushions with her hands fisted on her hips. A paramedic squatted in front of her, leaning forward to keep the ice pack on the back of her neck.

"You were shot!" Aneta said, eyes wide.

"With a Lemon Bomb!" Sunny said. "Who knew candy could

make such a bump!"

The paramedic removed the ice pack so Esther could feel where the sting had started. A nasty welt that felt three inches high, but probably wasn't, raised from her skin. She knew Lemon Bombs. They were a marble-shaped hard lemon candy. *Hard* candy. They were too sour for her. But how did she get hit with candy?

She moved her head. *Ow.*

Her mother smoothed the hair away from her forehead.

"I got hit with *candy?*"

"I thought you were dead when you fell over!" Aneta was kneeling next to the couch, patting Esther's knee.

"I fell over?"

"The paramedics think you might have passed out for a minute."

"Passed out?" She sounded like a parrot, not like the magnificent Bubo, who was high in the sky or a tree right about now.

"Yeah, and you missed Cat's launch!" Vee spread her arms out like wings and lifted them to the ceiling.

Not necessarily. Vee would argue with her that she couldn't have seen it if she'd been knocked out. *But I know I did.*

Someone brought her a glass of water. Taking a few thirsty gulps—getting hit with a Lemon Bomb made a person thirsty—the pieces began to fall into place. All except for one. The voice saying, *"I had no idea she would. . ."*

The paramedics packed up, reassured Esther's parents that she did not have a concussion but would have a nasty bruise for quite a while, and departed in their truck. The parents walked outside with Byron and Beverly, leaving the girls in the sitting room. With the girls circled on the floor in front of her, Esther felt special. They *cared* about her.

"Who was that voice that said something about 'she'?" she asked, reaching back and touching the welt again. "Why did Byron say, 'Unbelievable'?"

"Crazy." Sunny shook her head. "It was crazy."

"She didn't mean to hit either of them," Aneta jumped in. "It was because of the bird show we went to."

"She only meant to scare them away from her uncle's chicken farm," Vee added. "And her uncle loves Lemon Bombs, so she had plenty to use."

Sunny took over. "Except they weren't the ones bugging the chickens."

"I heard Todd Hudson tell your dad, Esther, that she's 'fifteen, but. . ,' whatever that means." Aneta shrugged.

The candy knot on Esther's neck must have swizzled her brain. "What?" she asked, widening her eyes and shaking her head as if to clear it from incoherence. "Who?"

The three talked at once, until Esther yelled, "Hey!" Sunny and Aneta told Vee to give the details in her direct way.

The facts were, Esther at last was able to determine, that Todd Hudson the chicken farmer had a sister who lived in Eugene. Her husband was serving in Afghanistan, and their daughter was struggling with her dad away. So Todd suggested the girl visit him for a while. Her "special" school gave permission, Aneta put in.

"She went to the same bird show we did then heard her uncle complaining about 'those birds' hitting on his chickens."

"She thought it must be the Beake birds because they lived near the chicken farm." Sunny couldn't stand not to participate.

"That's the sabotage. She thought Byron was letting them out and *sending* them to the chicken farmer. So she was going to let them out to fly away."

"Okay. Last question then. What about the night-vision goggles and the slingshot?"

"Her dad and she used to play in their backyard with the

night-vision goggles. She wouldn't leave home without them. They would shoot cans off picnic tables with their slingshots."

Esther rolled her eyes. "And I thought it was Melissa. It was a whole *story*." She gingerly touched the back of her neck.

What an adventure. Living the yayness.

Chapter 28

Launching Esther

A week later, since Beverly said she needed time to make it "grand," a tent like people used for weddings stood covering a great deal of the backyard between the mansion and the carriage house. The dining room table was outside, too, covered in a heavy white tablecloth. China and silverware and fresh flowers in crystal vases. Additional tables were at right angles to the main table, so it made a U shape.

Esther couldn't wait until Beverly gave the signal. Then she would give the girls her gift for their bracelets. To remember her. Her throat tightened. *It's not like you're leaving tomorrow.*

"Wow." Esther's dad stopped just outside the back door of the mansion. He shifted Siddy to his other arm. "Lots of breakable things."

"Lots of breakable things!" Siddy shouted back.

"Dad would like Siddy to be careful," her dad said, setting the three-year-old down, retaining a grip on Siddy's hand. Toby wandered off to see C.P., who was wearing a button-up shirt and a tie. Unbelievable.

"DAD WOULD LIKE SIDDY TO BE CAREFUL!"

Esther spotted the Squad over by the food table where—she

gasped—an ice sculpture of a great horned owl in flight stood in the center. A punch bowl flanked the owl on either side, and tiny cups encircled them. She raced over to the girls, feeling her new green dress flitter around her knees. She'd never much liked dresses, but when Beverly Beake asked if it were all right if they had a dress-up celebration of Esther's daring rescue of Bubo/Cat/Legs/Socko, the girls had clapped their hands and shrieked yes! Esther clutched a small brown paper bag.

"For pizza sake, can you believe this?" Sunny spun in a soft, sky-blue dress with a lace shrug. Esther had never seen her in a dress. She looked, well, like Sunny in a dress. Her unruly hair was piled on top of her head, with a few tendrils floating down. Sunny would always be Sunny no matter what she wore and where she went. Esther hoped this was true of herself, too.

"An ice sculpture that looks like Legs!" Aneta reached up and stroked the line of the outstretched wing. Her scarlet satin dress, with a short-sleeved black jacket over it, made her look old enough to be a seventh grader. Esther paused before telling her this. In a few short months, they *were* going to be seventh graders. Just not together. She squared her shoulders. She had told herself in the mirror in her bedroom that she was *not* going to cry.

"I wonder if the wings will fall off if the shoulders melt first." Vee squinted at the owl. "It could happen." She wore a black dress that hung straight from her shoulders to above her knees with black velvet flats with red bows. Her hair was held back by a pearl headband. She looked smart and pretty, Esther thought. Behind her back, Vee was holding something that looked like a brown paper bag.

"This is so exciting," Esther remarked as Beverly called them all to their place cards at the three tables. It was a full backyard. Sunny's family was there, and C.P. had ridden with them. Frank and Nadine smiled at them. Vee's mom and Bill were there as well as the Twin Terrors and Vee's stepmom. Vee's dad was in Tokyo on business. Vee's mom looked so happy. Vee would make a great big sister. Esther knew these things.

The girls muffled their shrieks again when black-suited servers came out with covered plates—like a fancy restaurant—and the dinner began. Esther caught Byron's eye. Wearing a suit and pulling at his tie, he was across the table and down a couple of chairs. He winked. At least she thought he did, but maybe it was the light from the glowing white paper lanterns strung around the interior of the tent.

After dinner was over, the dessert of strawberries and Devon cream served and enjoyed, and dishes removed, Byron Beake rose.

"Beake Man!" the girls chorused.

He bowed. Tugging at his dress shirt collar, he thanked everyone for coming. "I would like to thank the S.A.V.E. Squad for being who they are—loud, determined, and thinkers of good ideas."

That is us! thought Esther, trading grins with the other Squaders.

Parents groaned then clapped heartily.

"The girls helped me see that being angry at all people for what a few did to me and to the animals is not wise. So, thank you, girls." He motioned to his sister who sat across the table from him.

Beverly Beake stood and walked around the table until she was standing next to her brother. "We saw the owl with many names very early this morning." She turned to smile at the girls, each of whom turned bright red.

"I still can't believe we all named the same owl!" Sunny muttered into her white cloth napkin.

"Yes, and that we were wrong about who would stay," Aneta whispered.

"He appears to be settling in the far meadow of Dave's ranch."

The older woman slipped her arm around her brother. "And now the S.A.V.E. Squad would like to make some presentations." Beverly waved to the girls and strode back to her seat.

It was only her, Esther thought, but that must be the signal. She stood up. So did Sunny, Aneta, and Vee. They tipped their heads, surveyed the brown paper bags, and giggled. Squaders thinking alike.

"Who goes first?" Vee asked.

"I will." Esther pulled three small tissue-paper-wrapped parcels from the bag and handed one to each girl. "Okay, I promised myself I wouldn't cry, so I'm going to talk fast. I love being in the Squad"— *Could she get through this?*—"and now I know that wherever I go, I will still be a Squader. So, Sunny, Aneta, and Vee, this is to remind you of our final mission."

"Ready—," Vee began.

"Set." Sunny spun in her excitement.

"Go!" Aneta shouted.

They ripped off the paper and began jumping up and down. Even Vee. A bead with the front of the great horned owl for each of them. Esther had even bought one for herself. Just to keep it Squadish.

"We love it!" they shouted and smothered Esther with hugs. The four sat down and hurriedly untied their Squad leather string bracelets, sliding on the new owl bead. Esther began to tie up hers again.

"Wait, Esther." Sunny nudged her with an elbow.

"Now it's our turn." Sunny motioned to Vee. "One for each of us."

Vee removed four boxes from the paper bag.

Aneta and Sunny passed them around.

"Ready. . .go!" Esther could wait no longer. Holding her breath, she opened the box. On the cotton lay four red heart beads, each with the name of one of the S.A.V.E. Squad in white. The tears gushed out even as she reminded herself not to break her rule. *I'm going to miss them so much.* Again, she was surrounded.

"You're taking our hearts with you." Sunny's voice wobbled. "We each have all four hearts."

"So we will have your heart here with us." Aneta was weeping.

"So we are the S.A.V.E. Squad—f–forever!" Vee swallowed hard and began to slide the beads onto her bracelet. The other three scrambled to do the same.

Clenching her fist, Vee raised her arm. "S.A.V.E. Squad forever?"

Sunny, Aneta, and Esther met her fist with theirs, four bracelets touching. Strong. *Forever.*

Four strong voices that quavered at the end. "S.A.V.E. Squad for*ever!*"

The one who has to go will go. Esther smiled through blurry eyes. *To live the yayness.*

Lauraine Snelling is an award-winning author with more than seventy-five published titles including two horse-themed series for kids. With more than three million books in print, Lauraine still finds time to create great stories as she travels around the country to meet readers with her husband and rescued basset Winston.

Kathleen Wright was "Mrs. Write" to her Christian homeschoolers, ages ten to seventeen, whom she taught for many years. When she's not dreaming up adventures for her characters, she's riding bikes with her husband, playing pickleball, and trying to convince her rescued border collie that Mom knows best.